Once Upon a Woven Wish

An Enchanted Realms Novella

MICHELLE MILES

Rovenheim
Castle
venheim
Village
Malvina's
Fortress
Grimbrande
Mountains
ROVENHEIM
GEFGL
IDGE
o m
Ravenfell
Manor
Woodhaven
Kingdom
ONEBRIDGE

THE
FROEZEN
SEA
SNAE
Snow
King Leonidas
MER
Stonemere
Ariadne's Hidden
Tower
ean

To everyone who's made a wish at a fountain, blown out birthday candles, or tossed a penny into a well...this one's for you.

Chapter 1

Stonemere Village, Kingdom of Ebonvale, Gefglimmer Realm

The Well of Wishes had long since run dry. Its stones crumbled beneath moss and ivy, and its magic, if it ever had any, faded with the last of the old kings. Yet, when Serena knelt beside it, her hands shaking and her breath curling in the cold twilight, she offered her wish anyway.

A foolish hope, perhaps. But foolish hopes were all she had left.

The taxman would arrive at dawn. The greedy king had already taken so much. How much more would he take? Her family and the village were starving. Her father was sick, possibly dying. They had nothing left to give. No heirlooms. No livestock. No harvest. Just hunger, and hope fraying at the edges.

The mountain village on the edge of the kingdom was on the brink of ruin. It wasn't just her and her family. It was all of them.

The old tales spoke of a magical wishing well with the ability to grant one's heart's desire. Anything the wisher wanted. So, Serena sought the well, searching through dense forest until she found it hidden beneath overgrown ivy and weeds, concealed to all but the most keen.

Or the most desperate.

It had taken her all afternoon to clear the overgrowth. Her gown was soiled and sweat-stained, her hands raw. Every muscle ached from the effort. Hunger pangs plagued her. She had a desperate thirst. But peering down into the well, she saw nothing. No glisten of dark water. Only stones and sprouts of weeds pushing through the mortar.

Now, with the cold wind biting through her and the frigid ground seeping into her knees, she took a deep breath, ready to make her wish.

"I wish..." Her breath plumed in the air around her.

She paused, her mind frozen. What *was* her wish? Money for the taxman? Food for the table? To cure her sick father?

There were so many needs and only one wish. At least, according to the legend.

She closed her eyes against the night, shivering in the cold breeze, and placed her hands on the edge of the crumbling stone well.

"I'd give anything to save them," she whispered.

A desperate plea in desperate times. The wind stilled. Silence descended. And for a long, quiet moment, there was nothing. No response.

It was worth a try, even though she failed. She rose on shaking legs, her hands ice cold.

"I tried," she said and turned away. It was a long trek back to the village, and night was upon her.

"What will you pay?"

The man's voice curled like thread spun from the night. Cold. Mysterious.

She turned back to see him standing there, cloaked in shadows. He wore black. His face was hidden in the night.

A shiver danced up her spine. She took a step back, clutching her elbows, her worn boots crunching on the bracken.

"Who are you?"

"You called me, did you not?"

"I called no one. I-I made a wish."

"All wishes are calls. The Well remembers them all." He smiled. Not a warm smile. Not a smile that reached his eyes.

She looked past him toward the empty stone overgrown with brush.

"The well is dry," she said.

"That doesn't mean it's dead."

He moved closer, stepping into the fading light of day streaming through the treetops. His alabaster skin, glistening with an otherworldly glow, looked as though it had been carved from marble. Perfect. Flawless. With high cheekbones, a wide forehead, and curved pink lips. Beneath the hood of his cloak, his startling green-blue eyes peered back at her with curiosity. He was dressed all in black with a black cloak wrapping around him, the tail fluttering in the faint breeze.

He had simply appeared before her. She sensed something ancient about him, though she could not say what it was.

"I can grant you whatever you wish," he said softly. "Pay your debts. Feed your village. Cure your father. Whatever you need."

Her heart drummed hard, hope rising within her. It was as though he looked into her soul and saw her most desperate needs. All her wishes could come true. He held them in his hands, and all she had to do was say the word.

But—

"At what cost?" she asked, wary.

He raised one gloved hand and tapped her chest above her heart with the tip of his finger. "A part of you. The Well decides."

A shudder went through her as she peered at the stranger. He wanted a piece of her. What did that mean? She shook her head.

"I have nothing to give."

A smile split his face. "Even the poorest soul carries something worth taking."

Her gut clenched. Her breath caught. "Like what?"

"You have a name. A voice. A story. Memories. Dreams. Hopes. Secrets." He tilted his head. "Anything can be spun from a single memory."

She clutched her elbows tighter. "You...want my memories?"

He shook his head. "I don't. The magic does. The Well does. I only collect." His words were thin, tired. Fatigue lined his features.

"And if I say no?"

"Your father dies. The taxman takes all you have. And you will not survive the winter."

Harsh, she thought. The wind moaned between them, an ominous portent. Serena dropped her hands and gazed down at them. Pale. Chapped. Worn. She worked them hard to keep her family from starving. Anguish pounded through her. And here was this man ready and willing to grant her every wish.

For a price.

She drew in a long breath, expelled it in a shuddering plume. If she gave a piece of herself away, would it be worth it? Would they survive?

"I'll do it." Her words were quiet.

A soft smile touched his lips. "Then make your wish, Serena Windriver."

Her blood ran cold. She had not given him her name. Yet he knew. Or perhaps the magic in the well knew. She cut a glance at the old well sitting dark and silent as if waiting and watching.

Serena made her wish before dawn under a moonless sky with a cold winter wind ruffling her untidy hair.

She told herself it need not be extravagant.

"I wish for enough money to pay the taxes and keep our home."

She expected something fantastical to happen. But nothing did. No lightning. No ominous howl of the wind.

The man stepped back to the edge of the well. He removed his gloves, revealing skin inked with glowing symbols shimmering faintly like ancient runes that no longer had names. They spiraled from his fingers, curled around his wrist, and disappeared in the sleeve of his black tunic. He reached his gloveless hand to the well, holding it over the opening and whispering strange words in a language she didn't know.

Golden light danced upward from the well, swirling around his hands. His fingers bent, closing as though gripping the light itself. Then, the air twisted and split, tearing open for a heartbeat before closing again.

But Serena saw it.

The world split like a woven cloth unraveling, long enough for this man to draw something out. A sprinkle of shadow and starlight between his fingers. He cupped the light in his hand, cradling it as though it were something fragile. He brought his other hand up, both hands moving with impossible grace, weaving a strand of light. The air glimmered.

Then, shimmering like spider silk, threads looped through his fingers. Shaping. Morphing. Creating.

Gold.

Strands. Then curls. Then, circles turned into coins. Clinking softly onto the rim of the stone well.

Shining. Bright. Real.

He continued to work, creating more weavings of light that turned into more round gold coins. When he finished, a bulging satchel rested at her feet.

"Enough, you said. Enough and no more." His voice was laced with exhaustion as he sagged against the old well. Tired lines creased his face as though weaving the wish took a toll.

Perhaps it had.

Serena's eyes burned with the hot sting of tears. "You...did it."

He said nothing, his face remaining impassive.

She started to thank him, but then a wave of dizziness accosted her. She swayed on her feet, a flutter rising in her chest. She touched her head as she reached out to steady herself on the stone of the well.

He moved back, putting distance between the two of them.

A strangeness overcame her.

"What—" But the word stuck in her throat. She blinked, her vision fuzzy.

There was a thought at the edge of her mind that was now gone. She placed a hand to her temple and rubbed.

"The price has been paid," he said, his voice solemn.

"What did you take?"

"A memory," he said.

Panic seized her. "What memory?"

"If you knew, it would not be gone." His mouth drew down in a frown as though sorry for the taking. "You will remember the wish. Always. But the cost...it leaves space."

She pressed cold, shaking fingertips to her lips. What had she done?

"I want it back." Her voice warbled with her fear, her regret.

"No refunds."

A choked sob escaped her. She turned to hide her shame, putting her face in her hands as the hot tears pricked her eyes.

"Now, go," he said.

When she turned back, he was gone. Only the satchel of gold remained.

But beneath her skin, shimmering under the surface, was a tremor of something forgotten. Something changed. She would never be the same.

Chapter 2

S he half-ran, stumbling once on a rock, but didn't stop. The well's memory clung to her like fog. She kept seeing his eyes. Hearing his voice. *What will you pay?* With the weight of the satchel clutched between her hands, her heart raced. Not only from the exertion of the climb but also from the sheer fear pounding through her from her experience at the well.

When she exited the edge of the woods, she paused to see the village in the distance. Quiet, sleepy. Not yet alive with the raucous noise of village life.

Dawn was burning on the horizon. Which meant the taxman would come to collect his debts soon. How was she to get the satchel into the village without garnering attention? By the time she arrived, the first stirrings would be happening. It was heavy, bulging and noticeable.

Serena chewed her lower lip, unsure of her next move. She had no choice and needed to get there before he came calling.

Taking a deep breath, she headed down the footpath once more. After trudging the long way, she made it to the edge. The sun rose higher in the sky and there, on the edge of the village, was the sheriff's familiar carriage.

She swallowed hard. Whose house was he in? The Brightwood's? The Fullhide's? Hornraven? Not wanting to linger, she forced her feet to move and hurried into the village. As she neared her small home, the door to the Hornraven home burst open. Mrs. Hornraven ran out sobbing, her face red and splotchy. Her cheeks were stained with tears. Mr. Hornraven followed, carrying the smallest child. Their two other children were on either side of him.

And then, stepping out after them, the taxman and the sheriff. Urbano Lackman strutted like he owned the village, his greasy hair matted to his head, that familiar sneer plastered on his face. Cold. Heartless. He was glad to see them thrown out. She could feel it. He craned his neck and looked up at the home that was barely more than a hovel. But it was all the Hornravens had.

"That should cover it," he said to the sheriff.

"We paid what we could," the woman sobbed. "Please! Please, I beg you. Give us more time."

Her husband was at her side, reaching for her arm and tugging her toward him with a gentle nudge.

"No extensions," the man said, his tone cold and unrelenting. "King's orders."

Guilt bloomed in her chest like fire. *It's them. Not us. Not today.* That truth cut worse than any blade. The oldest boy's face was devoid of emotion. The middle girl clutched her doll, all she had left, as giant tears rolled down her face. The man was red with fury but said nothing, for he knew the punishment for speaking out against the king's men.

"Where are we supposed to go?" Mr. Hornraven asked.

The taxman shrugged. "Don't know. Don't care." Then to the sheriff, "Next house!"

He knocked on the Fullhide's door while Mrs. Hornraven continued to wail.

Serena fled, eyes down. She didn't look back. She didn't want to see another family fall. Her front door clicked shut behind her, and only then did she let herself breathe.

As soon as the door closed, she heard a deep cough coming from her father. Her younger sister, Maris, came from the bedroom with an expectant expression.

"Where have you been? Papa has been asking for you."

Serena pulled the edge of her threadbare cloak closer to hide the satchel of gold. She hurried through the small cabin to the room she shared with her sister.

"I had an errand," she called.

"An errand? For what? Today is tax day, Serena. How are we—"

"I know," she said, cutting her off. She half-turned to look at her over her shoulder. "I'll handle it."

"But—"

Serena closed the bedroom door, cutting her off. She stood for a moment in the solace of the room, closing her eyes and taking a long, cleansing breath. She was trying to make sense of what she'd done. What she'd seen. And what it might cost her. She hurried to her narrow bed and dumped the satchel. Coins clinked, forming a golden mountain. Quickly, she counted, knowing she needed three hundred for the taxes.

When she surpassed three hundred and went all the way to a thousand, her fingers trembled. She'd asked for enough. But this...this was too much. Why? Was it a mistake? A trap? Or something worse? The man's voice echoed again. *What will you pay?* Her breath hitched. What had she already paid?

A pounding on the door startled her. She scooped the money back into the satchel and stashed it under her pillow.

"Serena? He's here," Maris called through the door.

She smoothed her hair, but her palms were slick with sweat. She must remain calm. Smile. Lie, if she had to. She opened the door.

"Go tend Papa."

"But—"

"Now. Let me handle it."

Another pounding on the door. When her sister failed to move—her eyes ringed in fear—Serena gave her a gentle nudge toward their father's bedroom. Once the door was closed, she greeted the sheriff and taxman.

The sheriff looked tired, haggard, annoyed. The taxman, though, had a gleeful gleam in his dark eyes. She hated him all the more for it.

"Wait here," she said before he spoke.

Serena scurried back to her room and grabbed the satchel, then she returned with her head held high.

"For our taxes." She handed over the bulging bag.

He took it, peered into it, likely doing a quick count. Then he looked back at her with narrowed eyes.

"What trickery is this?" he asked.

"What do you mean?" Her heart rammed against her ribs. "It's the gold you asked for. Payment in full."

"This is more than what's owed," he snapped.

At that, the sheriff leaned over to peer down into the bag. His eyes went wide at the amount of gold there.

"I know." Her voice was stronger than she had expected. "How much for the Hornraven family's debt?"

He studied her. Perhaps a little suspicious or a little impressed. She didn't know which.

"You're paying for them?"

She nodded. "I am."

He named the sum. She didn't react, didn't move a muscle. But the amount was far more than she expected.

"Then that should be enough," she said.

He stared at her, as though he wanted to object, but didn't.

"Very well."

He spun on his heel and stalked away from the door. The sheriff lingered there a moment longer, confusion on his face, before he turned and left, too.

Only when the door shut did she feel a tug beneath her breast. Pulling, as though something came loose. She staggered back, gripping the edge of the table. The tug beneath her ribs was sharp, aching. Like a thread yanked loose from her soul. She gasped, clutching the table. *Something's gone.* A song? A name? A face? She reached for it, but it was already dust.

The door to her father's room opened, and Maris stepped out, her wide-eyed gaze going from Serena to the closed front door and back again. Question was written all over her face.

"The taxes...?"

"Paid," Serena said, her tone calm and steady. Much calmer than she felt.

Maris's eyebrows drew together. "But how?"

"I told you before I would find a way, and I did."

Her heartbeat increased as she thought of the mysterious man and the wishing well. She did not dare tell her sister about either, or her father, because she didn't want to have to explain how it was even possible that he made her wish come true.

Maris had more questions, but her father called from his bed.

"Find Papa something to eat," Serena said.

Maris huffed, but she ignored her and entered the room, trepidation skittering through her.

Her father was propped up on the pillows of his bed. His arms resting by his side, the blankets tucked underneath them. His face was deathly pale, eyes closed, lips pressed together. A sheen of sweat beaded his forehead. His dark hair was plastered against his head.

The room smelled of death.

She hated it.

She hated seeing her father succumb to the sickness that had plagued him these last few years.

She forced her feet to move to his bedside and perched on the edge of the chair beside him. Her hand shook as she reached for his, patting his cold, clammy skin. She wanted to recoil, but forced herself to hold his hand. To give him the comfort he needed. To know he was not alone.

His eyes fluttered open and fixed on her. A weak smile creased his pale lips.

"Serena, dear girl. There you are."

A cough wracked his frail body, his chest rattling with consumption.

A pang went through her, making her chest tighten.

"How are you feeling today?" It was a rhetorical question. One she did not expect him to answer.

He wheezed as he tried to answer. She reached for the damp rag to wipe his brow. The water in the bowl was murky. Annoyance flashed through her. Maris did not freshen the water.

When her sister pushed open the door, Serena looked up. The girl carried a wedge of stale bread.

"This is all we have left."

Serena took it from her, holding it in her hand as she reached for the bowl.

"Take this. Refresh the water from the well. Bring clean linens," she ordered, her voice terse.

Maris frowned. "But I haven't slept all night. And I'm hungry," she whined.

She was hungry too, but she didn't whine about it. She was tired too, but she forced herself to go on.

"Do as you're told," she snapped. "Then you can rest."

With a pout, she snatched the bowl from her hands and stalked out.

"Don't be so hard on her," Papa said, his voice weak. "She's all you have left."

Serena placed the bread aside. She stood and slid an arm behind him, lifting him enough to fluff the pillows.

"I still have you."

He coughed again as he leaned into the pillows. Serena busied herself with arranging his blankets to ease his discomfort.

Maris stomped into the room again with the bowl of fresh water and clean linen rags. She gave her a nod of thanks before the girl scurried off to their bedroom to rest.

"Serena..." He gasped her name, his voice raspy. "I do not have much time." He closed his eyes, leaning heavily into the pillows.

Fear stabbed her heart. "Don't talk like that. You'll be—"

"No. Sit, please."

With her heart clawing its way to her throat, she sat, her hands clasped in her lap to keep them from shaking.

"How about some bread?" she asked.

He shook his head, a slow movement from side to side. "No. Tell me a story."

"A story?"

"Yes. When your mother lived...the flowers were in bloom. I can see the flowers in bloom and smell their sweet scent."

He was delirious. She searched her memory for that time, but came up empty.

"I'm sorry, Papa. I don't remember that."

He wheezed again, trying to draw in a breath. His eyes cracked open as he looked at her and smiled.

"You were eight. Maris was four. Your mother wove flower crowns for festival day for both of you. Flowers from her garden. You wore pink. Maris wore yellow. Dresses your mother made."

His eyes fluttered closed, as though speaking was an effort. He grew quiet then, falling asleep at last.

As he did, Serena searched her memory for the flower crowns and the garden and the festival he talked so fondly of. She had no memory of it, as though there was nothing but a black void there.

While he slept, she rose from the chair and crept from the room. She hurried to the one she shared with her sister, her steps light on the wood floor.

Maris slept, curled on her side. Serena stood there for a long moment, unsure what she was searching for.

Her gaze swept the room. Her sister's boots, the cracked windowpane, the faded ribbon tied to the bedpost. Familiar things.

But something inside her had shifted. The well had taken something. Left a hole she couldn't fill. She clenched her fists at her sides. One wish. One family saved.

How many more would it take before she forgot who she was?

CHAPTER 3

The afternoon waned. Her father's condition worsened. He was in pain as he coughed up blood.

Serena sat beside him, her gut clenched with worry. Her sister paced the short length of the cabin outside his bedroom door. Her footsteps shuffled in a rhythmic way that started to grate on Serena's nerves. But Maris did not know how to deal with this sort of thing. She was never good with the sick or the injured. She preferred to hide and let Serena deal with it.

When their mother died, she did the same.

Serena had always been the strong one. The one to see after everyone. The one to take care of Maris and her father. She worked the herb garden. She hunted for pelts to trade. She baked the bread and did everything she could to keep food on the table.

And now she had made a sacrifice to keep them in their home. She'd paid the taxman. She'd helped the others in the village.

But now that the end was near for her father, a sense of helplessness shifted through her. He was so sick, and he was dying. There had to be something she could do.

There *was* something she could do.

Her body stilled as she sat up ramrod straight in the chair, her hands clasped in her lap as the thought shifted through her mind. Dare she? Should she? Could she?

She had to. It was the only way to save him.

She shoved up from the chair. Her father coughed again. She held the kerchief to his mouth. It came away speckled with blood, sending a stabbing pain right to her heart. She was unwilling to lose her father, too.

She reached for the cup of water on the side table and helped him take a sip.

"You're going to be all right, Papa," she murmured.

His eyes fluttered closed as he leaned back into the pillows, as though it were an effort. He released a shuddering breath between his dry, cracked lips.

She hated seeing him this way. She leaned down, kissed his forehead. One last look at him and then she turned away. Maris stopped her incessant pacing as Serena barreled out of the room and grabbed her cloak off the hook by the door.

"Where are you going?" Panic laced her sister's voice.

"To fetch the doctor," she lied. "I'll be back. Watch over him."

A choked sob escaped her. "Serena, I can't—" Her breath hitched, her voice rising in dread.

She turned to her and gripped her by the arms, giving her a little shake. "You can. Stay here with him. He needs you. Do not leave his side. Do you promise?"

Maris chewed on her lower lip. Her glassy eyes were wide and shimmery.

"Promise?" Serena demanded.

Her sister nodded. "I promise."

"I'll be back soon."

Serena was out the door before Maris could reply. She knew her sister did not want to be there alone when—if—their father passed. But she had no choice.

There was only one person who could help.

The girl returned. He sensed her long before he saw her.

Why had she come back?

Certainly not for another wish. He could not grant her another. Could not take another piece of her. Though he knew if he granted her wish, the price would have to be paid. And he would have no choice.

He was bound to obey the laws of magic, no matter how he felt about it. Or her.

She crested the hill, her feet swift on the footpath. She carried a lantern in the gloaming, the pale light flickering across her face, splashing in slashes across her worn clothes and scuffed boots.

The hood on her threadbare cloak fell back, revealing her halo of auburn hair in the faint light. She halted the moment she saw him standing by the well.

Her blue eyes went wide. Her mouth formed a silent O as she stifled a gasp. She did not expect to see him there. Waiting for her.

Hoping to see her once again.

"You," she breathed. Her breath plumed white in the chilly air. "You're here."

He wanted to tell her to go back home. To leave him in this place, leave him with his solitude and his loneliness. And yet, here she was with her wide eyes full of hope. Hope she knew he could give her.

For a price.

"I am," he said, his voice quiet in the night. Though he tried to refuse the burning magic within him, he added, "What is your wish?"

"You know I came for another?" She held up the lantern and moved closer, the light bathing her features in a soft glow.

Gods, she was beautiful.

Her face was delicate. High cheekbones. Full lips. Wide eyes fringed in dark lashes. Hair the color of spun silk pulled back at the nape and tied with a faded ribbon. Pale freckles dotted her nose and upper cheeks.

He wanted to refuse her. He knew he could not.

And he would regret taking another part of her if she made another wish.

"It is the only reason for your return, is it not?"

She pressed her lips together and nodded. "Yes, of course. I wish—"

"What did you do with the gold?" he interrupted, though he wasn't sure why he asked.

He wasn't ready for her to make her wish, to take another little piece of her. He wanted her to remain a moment longer, as herself. Looking at him with those bright, blue eyes full of hope. If only to assuage the hollowness burning in his chest.

He'd given her more than enough gold as a test. To see if she would squander it away on herself. To see if she was selfish like others. But she hadn't, had she? Judging by her appearance, she had not. She still wore the scuffed, worn boots and the threadbare cloak. Her face was pale, thin, gaunt. As though she had not had a proper meal in days.

So, what, then did she do with the extra gold he'd spun for her?

She blinked in surprise, taken aback by his abrupt question. "The gold?"

The magic inside him allowed him to only grant wishes, not question the wisher. Though with her arrival, something had shifted inside him. As though her presence cracked the surface and her vibrancy slowly seeped through.

He nodded. "It was more than enough, wasn't it?"

She flushed, her face going pale as she looked away. "I...I paid the taxman."

But he sensed she concealed something. The magic deep inside him shifted, cold tendrils reaching for the truth. "And?"

"For my family and…" She tugged her lower lip through her teeth. "Others."

"Others?" His brows rose. Shock rolled through him.

She kept her gaze downcast. "I paid for another family so they could keep their home."

Color bloomed high in her cheeks at her admission, as though she were afraid to tell him the truth. He gaped at her. She had used the extra not for herself, but for others in need. A piece of the magic inside him fractured a little more as guilt wracked him for taking her precious memory of her mother.

This was most unexpected.

And now she stood before him with another request. Not for herself, he'd wager. Though the magic within him would not allow him to refuse, the compassionate side of him wanted to tell her to go home.

A knot formed in his gut. His throat constricted. Try as he might, he was unable to stop from saying the words.

"What is your wish, Serena Windriver?"

She lifted her imploring gaze back to his. The lantern lit her face with hope. "My father. He's sick. Dying. Can you help him?"

Magic stirred within him. Ready to collect. "Of course, I can help him. What ails him?"

"When he coughs, there is blood," she said.

If he did not grant her wish, then her father would surely die. How could he refuse? "Speak the words and it will be done."

A pang of sorrow went through him. Because of what he would do to her when she said the words. That human part of him that barely existed. That he thought long dead. But there it was—alive. Surfacing. *Becoming*.

Because of her. Because he hated the price he'd have to collect from her.

"I wish for you to save my father. Please." As she said it, she clutched the lantern tighter in her hand, her knuckles leeched of color. As though she were afraid he would refuse.

He would not refuse.

"And so it will be done."

He removed his gloves, placing them aside on the crumbling stone, and lifted his hands to the Well. As before, light danced upward, swirling and curling around his fingers.

The runes carved along his skin from the cursed magic pulsed in their bright golden glow. The magic was stirring, creating, becoming deep inside him. And every time he chanted the words and brought it forth, it sent a searing pain through him.

Shimmering threads looped through his fingers as he thought of the girl's father lying sick and dying in his bed. Apprehension pulsed from Serena as she waited and watched him create the magic that would allow him to live. As the light danced up from the Well and it swirled about, it formed a glass bottle. Inside, the golden light shimmered and sparkled, danced and swayed, filling up the small bottle to the curve of its neck with its thick golden fluid. Then a cork sealed it.

And the magic finished.

He extended the bottle to her, his hand steady but his heart stuttering.

She hesitated, peering at it with doubt clouding her eyes. "What...is that?"

"An elixir. He drinks it," he said.

"And when he does, he's...cured?"

He nodded, watching and hoping she would not take it. She would not accept the magical gift and he would not have to take another piece of her.

But she reached for it. She slipped it from his hand, their fingers brushing for the briefest of moments, she likely didn't notice. But he did, and the touch burned through him, cutting him to the core.

Years had passed since he touched another.

And now, he'd touched her.

And everything had changed.

"Thank you," she whispered, her voice rough with emotion.

As she turned away from him, the light from her lantern splashed along the ground. He closed his eyes and claimed the magical price.

CHAPTER 4

Serena hurried back down the path from the well as night enveloped the village. In one hand, the lantern swung back and forth, lighting the way in a pale yellow glow. In her other, she clutched the small round vial with the cork, the substance inside shimmering with golden light.

Her labored breath turned to smoke in front of her, but she hardly noticed. Nor did she notice the cold seeping through her boots and cloak. Hope bloomed within her that this elixir would heal her father. That he would return to good health.

As she entered the outskirts of the village, though, she halted.

A strange sensation came over her. She saw stars as though she'd hit her head. She shook it, trying to understand what was happening to her. Her heart did a strange thump followed by an ache so deep, she doubled over. She still clutched the elixir in one hand, the lantern in the other. The lantern splashed light across her worn boots and for a moment, she didn't remember anything. Who she was. Where she was. Why she was outside in the darkness carrying a lantern. The bottle bit into her palm. She looked at it, a moment of confusion piercing her.

Her vision cleared as she sucked in a cold breath that stung her lungs. Then she righted herself and peered down at the row of houses in the small village ahead of her. Lamplight flickered in a few of the windows. The one on the end seemed familiar. It had rows of flowers along the dilapidated picket fence that was in desperate need of painting. Faded green shutters framed the windows and the red front door stood out in the shadows.

She tilted her head to the side, trying to recall why that was familiar. Another glance down at the vial in her hand.

Oh, yes. She went to see the wish maker. She asked him for...for...

She blinked, her brow wrinkling as she tried to pull the memory back.

She asked him to save her father. Yes, that was it.

Her father...who was sick and dying in his bed.

Her eyes landed on the small house with the faded green shutters and the red front door and it hit her. That was *her* house. That was where she was headed.

How strange she was unable to remember moments ago.

Serena shook it off and started down the path once again, into the village, toward her home. When she reached the red door, she jostled the vial, tucking it under her arm to grab the knob and fling it open.

Inside, the air was stuffy and smelled like sickness and...death. She kicked the door closed with the heel of her boot and set down the lantern on the floor. Maris popped out of their father's room, her eyes wide and round and full of hope. But the moment she saw her, hope faded from her face.

"Where's the doctor?" she asked. "Papa is worse—"

"He gave me this." She lifted the bottle. Inside, the golden liquid gleamed.

She shoved past her sister into the room and nearly gagged. The metallic tang of blood filled the air. Next to the bed, bloody rags. Her father, pale and sweating, propped against the pillows. His dark hair was plastered against his head. His lips were the color of snow. His breath was labored.

Maris followed on her heels. "What is that, Serena?"

She ignored her, as she pulled out the cork. Then she paused at her father's bedside, taking one of his hands. He was cold and clammy, his skin damp with fever. His eyes fluttered open as he looked up at her. He tried to smile, but it faltered.

"Serena..." His voice rasped as he squeezed her hand. "Where—"

"Shh, Papa. I have something that will help you."

She slid her arm around his back, easing him forward so he could drink. His gaze flickered to hers, uncertain but steady, filled with an abiding trust. In that moment, she felt the weight of it—that he relied on her for everything. The household, the debts, the meals. And more than that, he loved her.

"You've always been so strong," he muttered. "You have to keep being strong."

Her throat tightened. "I will. I promise, Papa. But now, you have to drink."

She pressed the bottle against his lips. He didn't resist. He swallowed the golden liquid until it was gone. Then he sank back into the pillows, exhausted.

Serena stepped back, the empty bottle slick in her hand, and watched as her father slipped into a gentle sleep. Relief should have followed—should have loosened the knot in her chest—but instead something colder threaded through her veins.

Maris appeared in the doorway, her eyes darting between their father and Serena. "Serena, is he—?"

"He should be fine now," she answered, though her voice came out clipped, distant.

She stared at her father, but the warmth she'd felt moments ago—the trust in his gaze, the love she'd been so certain of—drained from her. All she saw was a man who had leaned on her strength, who had demanded and demanded until she was nearly broken. And a treacherous thought took root. Would he ever thank her? Would he ever truly see her?

As the dark feelings bloomed inside her, something else flickered at the edges of her mind. A knowing. A sense of...what? That she had surrendered something. That she had agreed to a price as sharp and bitter as the metallic tang of blood in the air. That she had...lost something.

But she could not grasp what it was.

Maris edged closer, arms wrapped tight around herself. "When will we know?"

Serena tore her eyes away. "I don't know. Perhaps in the morning."

Weariness pressed down like a weight. She passed her sister the bottle and stumbled to her room, shedding her cloak where it fell. Boots kicked aside, she climbed onto the bed still dressed, sleep pulling her under like a tide.

The man lingered in the silence long after Serena's footsteps faded down the mountain path. The air stilled, heavy with damp stone and the faint shimmer of magic. He pressed his palms against the worn rim of the Well, staring into its depths where threads of light writhed like restless serpents.

Always the same. Another desperate mortal. Another bargain struck. Another piece of a soul unraveled to feed the Well's endless hunger.

But Serena was not the same.

Her eyes had burned with defiance, with love so fierce it threatened to undo her. He recognized it, though he wished he didn't. It was the same flame that had undone him centuries ago.

He remembered the girl. The mortal who had come to the Well weeping for her dying family. He had given her what she asked for, weaving her wish into warmth and life, defying the law that demanded payment. For a time, her joy had filled his dark world with light. But mortals were not meant to bear the weight of such magic, and in saving her family, he had doomed himself—and her laughter—to silence.

He had broken every law of his kin to save them. To save her. He had tried to bring her back when she was gone. That was his crime. His sin. His punishment.

The Fae High Court had bound him here, to the Well, chained to the magic he had twisted for love. Now he would grant wishes until his hands bled, until his heart turned to ash, until mortals walked away leaving him empty.

But still, he wove. Because he could not stop. Because that was his penance.

The laws were clear—grant a favor but take payment in return. A name. A memory. A feeling. It did not matter.

He dragged a hand down his face, shutting his eyes. Serena's voice still lingered in his ears, soft and certain, asking him to save her father. As he once begged to save the one he loved.

She would not thank him when the payment was due. None of them ever did. Yet when he thought of her, something sharp and dangerous stirred in him. A hope he had long since sworn dead.

"Don't be a fool," he muttered to himself, his voice rough in the night. "Not again."

But the Well rippled with starlight, and deep inside its waters, he heard her name whispered back to him.

Serena awoke to bright sunshine pressing against her eyes. For a moment, she remained where she was, nestled against her pillow and buried under the thin quilt her grandmother made. Maris had one like it.

But the room was too quiet. She didn't hear Maris snoring next to her, which was unusual. Maris was not an early riser. It was always Serena up early taking care of the household chores and making sure they weren't going to starve before next week.

Her eyes blinked open. Maris's bed was empty and unmade. As though she hastily got up, threw off the blankets. As if she'd leapt up in a hurry.

Serena sat up, straining her ears to listen. A man's voice, stronger than she remembered, joined by her sister's.

Papa.

Her breath hitched. She shoved aside the covers, swung her legs to the floor, and noticed absently the hole worn in the toe of her stocking. Something else to mend later. For now, she hurried from the room.

The door to her father's bedroom was cracked. She paused, hand braced on the frame, listening.

"...Serena went to the doctor," Maris's bright voice carried. "She came back late."

Serena pushed open the door. It swung open, banging against the wall, startling both of them. Gone was the sickly smell to the room. Now, the air was fresh and crisp. As though Papa had never been at death's door.

Papa sat upright against the pillows, the gray of sickness gone from his cheeks. His lips had color. His eyes shone. He looked—alive. More alive than she had seen in weeks.

But his smile—broad, crinkling his eyes—was fixed on Maris.

"You're up!" Maris said, hopping to her feet. Her voice was too high for the morning.

Her gaze flicked from her sister to her father, who smiled so wide his face lit with joy. But the smile wasn't for her. It was for Maris.

"Papa?" Serena whispered.

His eyes slid to her, but it was Maris he reached for, patting her hand where she perched beside him.

"Maris was letting you sleep in," he said warmly. "She told me how you stayed out late, fetching the doctor."

Maris flushed pink and ducked her head, her hands clasped tight. "It was nothing, Papa."

Nothing? Serena thought bitterly. She had climbed a mountain alone, carrying only a lantern. And yet here sat Maris, basking in his praise as though she'd been the one to do it.

"I did," Serena said. "Maris, fetch Papa some fresh water and whatever bread is left."

Her sister hesitated, reluctant to leave his side, but rose. She bent to kiss his cheek before slipping past Serena and hurrying to the kitchen.

Papa turned his eyes to Serena at last. He held out a hand, beckoning her closer. "Come, child."

She crossed to the bed, perched on the edge of the chair, and took his hand. His fingers were warm, strong. She searched his face, astonished at the change.

"Are you better?" she asked, tentative.

He nodded. "Whatever the doctor gave me worked. I should thank him."

"Oh," she said softly. "That's not necessary, Papa."

"Yes, it is," he insisted. "I hope you paid him properly."

"Of course," she murmured. Though the memory blurred in her mind. She remembered only the Well. The man. The golden elixir. Not how she had paid.

"Good." He slipped his hand from hers, already pushing aside the blankets. "Now, I'll get up. Too long I've been lying in this bed."

"What do you think you're doing?" she demanded, rushing to the other side.

"There's work to be done, Serena," he said firmly.

"No, Papa." Her voice sharpened. She placed her hands on his shoulders to give him a firm but gentle nudge. He sank back to the bed. "You should rest."

He opened his mouth, but Maris bustled back in with a cup of water and the last of the bread. "I brought this," she said. "It's all we have."

Papa's eyes softened as he looked at her. "You take it, my little dove."

Maris shook her head, cheeks pink. "No, Papa."

His stomach growled. Serena crossed her arms. "Eat it. Maris and I will be fine. I'll bake more bread, and I'll go hunting later."

"Hunting?" His brows shot up. "Since when do you hunt?"

Maris piped up helpfully, "She brought home rabbits once."

Papa gaped at Serena. "Rabbits?"

"Someone has to keep us fed," Serena said flatly, pressing the bread into his hands. "Rest today. Tomorrow you may help in the garden. It needs weeding before the first snows come."

He sighed but nodded, yielding. "Very well. Today, I'll rest. Tomorrow, I'll work."

Satisfied, Serena stepped back, letting Maris slip easily into the chair at his side once more. His attention turned to her, his smile reserved for her.

He had not thanked her for climbing the mountain in the dead of night. He had not thanked her for bringing back the elixir that saved his life. Instead, he smiled for Maris, let her kiss his cheek, let her laughter fill the room.

And Serena, standing in the doorway, felt the sharp, deep ache bloom inside her.

He favored Maris.

Now she told herself not to resent him. Not to resent either of them.

But the bitterness sat heavy on her tongue, impossible to swallow. Had she wished away her father's love? The question lodged deep inside her, sharp as glass, and she feared she already knew the answer.

CHAPTER 5

The days passed. The taxes were paid. Papa's strength returned. But Serena felt no peace. She baked, weeded, hunted—yet all the work only deepened the ache inside her.

But Serena felt a longing deep within she could not explain. As though something was missing. As though her soul was empty.

Her father was back to working a few hours a day in the garden wearing his oversized straw hat with the wide brim to keep the winter sun off his head and out of his eyes.

Her sister was back to whining about sweeping the floors, doing the washing, and mending the clothes.

While Serena worked long hours to make sure they remained unnoticed by the crown.

The villagers were abuzz about her father's miraculous recovery. When she was in town, Serena heard the whispers. Felt the curious sideways glances. One nosey woman hinted it was unnatural. Some credited the local doctor. Others claimed it was good luck, or perhaps a blessing.

The same luck or blessing that came with the gold Serena managed to get for the Hornraven's taxes and their own.

She knew, of course, the truth of it, but could say nothing about it. She could not tell them she made a bargain with the stranger at the Well of Wishes. A bargain that cost her... Well, she couldn't recall what it cost her. Something of herself? A memory, perhaps?

One bright morning, as Serena was kneading bread, a knock sounded on their door. Maris was busy sweeping their tiny living room while Papa was out back chopping firewood.

"Get that, Maris, will you?" She puffed a stray strand of hair out of her eyes as the knock sounded again.

Maris huffed. She dropped the broom and stomped to the front door. Though why she was annoyed about that was beyond her.

"Oh, hello, Dr. Graves," Maris greeted.

Serena froze, her heart clawing its way to her throat. Gods, the doctor must have heard about the *miraculous* recovery of their father and was coming to see how it was done. She pulled her hands out of the dough and reached for a kitchen towel, quickly wiping them.

"Hello, Maris. I came to see about your father."

Serena bustled toward the front door as the doctor pulled off his hat.

"He's doing fine, doctor," she said before her sister could chime in. "He's much recovered." She forced a smile that hurt her cheeks.

The doctor's eyes flickered to her, glinting with curiosity. "Yes, I've heard. Strange rumors in town, too, about that."

She nudged her sister out of the way, who huffed. "Oh?" she asked, trying to sound as innocent and curious as possible. "What sort of rumors?"

He cleared his throat, his face contorting in discomfort. "That, ah, it was a miracle."

Papa shuffled up to the door carrying an armload of firewood. The doctor heard him walk up and turned to greet him.

"Windriver," the doctor said with a nod. "You're looking well. Quite well, actually."

"John Graves! Haven't seen you about in ages."

A wide grin split her father's face as he headed past the doctor and into the house. He went to the hearth to drop the firewood. Maris had retreated to somewhere behind her. Hopefully out of earshot. Papa brushed the dirt from his hands and turned to face the doctor.

"What brings you out here?" he asked.

An innocent question enough but Serena stiffened.

"You, actually," he said, looking him over. He stepped inside the house, still clutching the brim of his hat between his tense fingers. "The last time I saw you, you were at death's door."

Papa laughed a deep hearty laugh. "Well, I suppose that's true. But your medicine did the trick."

"My...ah...medicine?" he asked.

"The elixir," Maris supplied helpfully, chirping from somewhere behind her.

Serena cringed. Confusion creased the doctor's face when he turned his gaze from Papa to her. As though she might have the answer. She continued to smile.

"What elixir?" the doctor asked.

"Why, the one you sent with Serena," Papa said. "Worked like a charm."

He looked so happy, so proud as he glanced at her but his gaze settled on Maris. Serena bit her lip to keep from saying anything.

"I don't recall giving Serena an elixir," the doctor said, eyeing her from his position near the door.

"Dr. Graves, I heard Mr. Brightwood took a fall the other day and twisted his ankle," Serena said, trying desperately to change the subject. "How is he doing?"

Graves was a bit taken aback. "I intended to look in on him after seeing about your father."

Serena muscled her way between Papa and the doctor, twisting the kitchen towel tight in her hands. She nudged him toward the open door. "Well, as you can see, he's quite healthy. Not only is he strong enough to chop firewood, but he's also been helping in the garden."

"The weeding," Papa said in agreement.

"And...you're all right, then?" The doctor looked back at her father.

"Quite so, though I admit the back is a bit stiff from all the work." He chuckled, as though he was glad to have the work instead of lying in bed all day.

Serena plastered in a bright smile and waved him toward the door. "There you have it, doctor! Thank you for coming by to check on him. We appreciate it."

He stepped out, his face a map of confusion. Serena braced a hand on the door, ready to push it closed.

"Please tell Mr. Brightwood we hope he's better," she said, her voice a little too high, a little too cheerful.

Dr. Graves nodded. "Good day to you then."

The doctor lingered a heartbeat too long, his gaze flicking from Serena's too-bright smile to Papa's ruddy cheeks.

"Strange," he muttered, mostly to himself before he tugged on his hat and walked away.

Serena blew out a breath of relief and closed the door. When she turned around, both Papa and Maris stared at her. Papa with a look of disdain. Maris with shock.

"That was rude," Maris said. "You hustled him out of here like he was a common thief."

Serena huffed out a forced laugh. "I did not."

Gripping the kitchen towel, she headed back to the kitchen.

"You did. I'll not have you treating the village folk like that, Serena," Papa said, his tone edged with disdain. "They mean well enough." Then to Maris, "Don't they, little dove?"

Her back stiffened as she glared down at the mound of half-kneaded dough. Neither of them had any idea what she went through to get that elixir. Climbing the mountain in the cold. Returning with it and losing...

...what? What did she bargain away?

She couldn't recall.

All she knew was Papa was disappointed with her and continued to favor Maris. Neither of them appreciated her.

"I'm sorry, Papa."

Without turning, she placed aside the towel and started back to work to finish the bread.

"See that it doesn't happen again."

He opened the door and stepped back out into the chill of the morning. She sensed her sister lingering behind her.

"You didn't get that elixir from the doctor, did you?" Maris asked, a note of accusation tinging her voice.

"I have work to do and so do you," was her only answer.

"But—"

"Back to work," she said, flashing a cold look over her shoulder. "The floors aren't going to sweep themselves."

Maris frowned, clearly hurt by her words which she instantly regretted. But she didn't want to answer any more questions about the elixir or Papa's illness.

Serena drove her fists into the pliant dough, the sticky air of yeast clinging to her skin. Was it a mistake to climb the mountain? To take the elixir? To trade away...

What?

The thought unraveled like a spool of thread, slipping through her fingers, leaving her hollow.

She straightened, jaw tight. No. It had been the right choice. Her family's survival demanded it. Let the whispers come. Let the doctor pry. She would endure it all.

Even if she had to go back to the Well.

CHAPTER 6

That night, moonlight filtered through the grime-covered window, cutting through the gossamer curtains that did nothing to shield the room from the slashes of light. Serena lay in her bed staring at the window, listening to the faint wind around the house. In the bed next to her, Maris slept with her back to her. They hadn't spoken again since she snapped at her.

She tried to apologize. But every time she tried, the words died on her tongue. Leaving behind ash and anguish.

And Papa. He was less than cordial through their evening meal. He kept the fire stoked and dozed by it in his favorite chair, his legs stretched out before him, a book open on his chest. She wanted to insist he go to bed, but she decided she'd done enough insisting for one day.

She rolled to her side, trying to close her eyes and sleep, replaying the events and regrets of the day.

And thinking about the stranger at the Well of Wishes.

Who was he? Did he have a name? Was his sole purpose to grant wishes and make bargains? What had he taken from her? Was it why she felt so...hollowed out? So lost? So alone?

Frustration edged through her. She shoved off the heavy quilt and slipped out of bed. Her bare feet hit the cold floor, sending a shiver up her shift. She cut a glance to her sister. She hadn't moved. She continued to sleep.

Serena moved about the room, quick and quiet. She pulled on her woolen dress, stockings, and grabbed her cloak. She swept her boots off the floor, stealing another glance at her sister.

Good. She was sleeping. Her breathing was heavy.

She crept out of the room on silent feet, closing the door behind her with a soft snick. A quick glance around the cabin to see the fire was nothing more than embers and her father's chair empty. He'd gone to bed.

At the door, she slipped on her boots and pulled the cloak tight around her thin frame. She picked up the lantern and opened the door.

The cold bit right through her well-worn cloak. But she ignored it as she closed the door behind her, then lit the lantern.

Her breath came in smoky plumes as her booted feet crunched on the newly fallen snow. And it was still snowing. Tiny flakes danced in the wind, fluttering down to the ground. By morning, it would be a thick blanket. She hoped to be back by then.

Every step she took was another step toward something danger-ous. But she *had* to know.

The lantern swung at her side, spilling light across the snow to light her way. Houses were dark. Gray smoke curled from chimneys. She should be in bed, buried beneath her quilts, sleeping like the rest of the village. But instead, she needed answers.

And the stranger was going to give them to her.

The climb up the mountain was never easy. Made even more difficult by the swirling snow. The embankment was slick with mud as she made her way up. But determination was stronger than turning back. Her breath misted in the chill. The lantern splashed golden light over the bracken not yet coated with snow.

As she approached, worry gnawed through her. Worry that she might lose a piece of herself once again to the stranger at the Well of Wishes. Echoes of her last two visits haunted her.

Make your wish, he'd intoned.

And she had looked into his green-blue eyes. Eyes that peered back at her with a mixture of curiosity, bemusement, and, perhaps, even regret.

She shoved aside branches as she made her way. The closer she got to the well, the thicker the air seemed to be. Oppressive silence pressed all around her. There were no nocturnal sounds here. She hadn't noticed that before.

As she crested the hill, she froze.

There, sitting on the edge of the well, was the stranger. His ungloved hands were making symbols in the air. Cool moonlight slashed through the treetops overhead, bathing in an ominous blue-white glow. He pulled shafts of light toward him, spun them into threads, and flung them skyward where they burst into sparks.

It was beautiful—and terrifying. A reminder of what he was, and what he had already taken from her.

As though he were practicing.

Or bored.

He never looked at her as he spoke. "Most mortals come only once. Twice if they're desperate. You must be *very* desperate, Serena Windriver."

"You..." Her breath fogged in the cold, ragged and uneven, and she lost all thought, all nerve.

She should turn around and go back home. Leave this strange man with his golden threads of magic to himself. He dropped his hands and turned to her, a look of bemused resignation on his handsome features. The hood still draped his head, hiding most of his face.

"Come for another wish?" he asked.

"No," she said, her voice terse.

He lifted a brow. "Curious. Then why are you—"

"You tricked me," she interrupted, her fury rising.

A faint smile lifted the corners of his lips. "You made a bargain, dear girl. All bargains come with a price. Which you paid."

A shudder went through her. "What did you take from me?"

"That I cannot tell you."

"Why not?"

He remained silent as he peered at her from across the way. Nothing between them but thick emotion and thicker silence.

Next to him, moonlight cast down into the well, illuminating the old moss-covered stones. Which seemed to shimmer.

"We struck a bargain. What's done is done," he said.

A half-formed memory floated through her mind. A crown of flowers. A woman's face—gentle and kind—and then it was gone when she tried to grasp it.

"But I-I can't remember." Her breath hitched, pluming once again in front of her. "I should remember."

"That's the nature of the thing," he said, his voice calm and even. "The Well takes what it will."

She balled her free fist. "You mean *you* take what you will."

The stranger's expression flattened. His eyes turned dark and dangerous. No longer were they hinted with amusement. "Every bargain cuts me too. Do you think I chose this?"

"Didn't you?"

He emitted a humorous laugh. "You know nothing about this," he waved toward the well, "or me."

Serena stepped a little closer, the lantern light catching his face. The air between them tightened, his expression carved from stone. His eyes hard and sharp. His jaw clenched tight.

"Do you stay here all night, all day, next to the Well, waiting for some pitiful mortal to come along and make a wish? So you can bargain away some precious piece of them—"

"I do as I am commanded," he snarled.

The words cracked like a whip and she jerked, as if struck. She shrank back, her heart skittering in her chest.

"You would be wise to return home, Serena Windriver, and never return."

Her name on his tongue struck a nerve deep within her. "You know my name but I do not know yours."

He pressed his lips together in a thin line. "It is no longer mine to give."

She sucked in a breath. "What does that mean?"

He turned away, reaching for his gloves on the side of the well and pulling them on. It occurred to her, then, that he did not seem affected by the cold. Nor did his breath plume when he spoke.

"A name is a lock, and the tongue that speaks it is the key."

She blinked, unsure what that meant. "I don't understand."

He huffed in annoyance. "I do not stay here, mortal, of my own free will. I cannot leave this place. This Well is my cage, and every wish my chain."

"You're...bound here?"

"Bound. Cursed. Use whatever word suits you. Go home, Serena," he said, again. There was a weariness in his tone, as though fatigue pounded through him with her demanding questions.

"No," she replied, determination and defiance pressing through her. "I want answers. I *need* answers. Tell me—"

"There is nothing to tell," he snapped. "Do you not understand? I pay, too."

The words slammed into her. Her anger snagged on a sudden jolt of doubt. His tone indicated he was not interested in further argument. Fire flashed in his green-blue eyes. He clenched his jaw, the muscles ticking along the edge.

"I...wanted to know what I lost."

Heat bloomed in her breast. A lump formed in her throat. Tears threatened. How could he be so cruel? How could he take what he wanted?

How could she let him?

"If you cannot name it, perhaps that's the cruelest part of all. Do you truly want to know?"

She nodded. "Yes. *Please*!"

His eyes glinted in the glow of the lantern. "Then climb again. Wish again. And learn your fate. A fate that will unravel you, body, mind, and soul."

She sucked in a breath. "But that will...ruin me."

His jaw clenched. "No. You'll ruin yourself." He turned his back to her. "Now, go back to the village. Do not return here unless you wish to tempt your fate once more."

The stranger, this wish giver, refused to look at her anymore. So she turned from him, clutching the lantern in her frozen hand as she started the long trek back home. Back down the mountain. Disappointment and frustration edged through her.

As she headed down the footpath, the snow came down harder, making it more and more difficult to walk. But she had to get home before the first light of day so as not to be missed.

The stranger's words shook her to the core. *Bound. Cursed. Use whatever word suits you.*

In that, they were alike. She, too, felt trapped. Trapped in a world that was of her own making. A world in which she lost something that was once precious to her, that once meant something. And now it was gone. Forever.

I pay, too.

His words haunted her all the way home.

Chapter 7

Winter came early. Snow blanketed the village, which was unfortunate because they had not yet harvested all they could from the Fall garden. Serena had a stack of animal pelts to trade in the village square. They needed provisions, but the snow was thick and still coming down.

She peered outside the window in the kitchen, watching it with dismay and worrying her bottom lip.

The start of it seemed to be when she had visited the stranger demanding answers.

She couldn't help but wonder if her desperate attempt to get the truth had angered him, and this was his retaliation. But that didn't make sense. He could no more control the weather than she could.

Could he?

The animal pelts were lined up by the front door. The rabbit stew was simmering in a pot on the stove filling their small cabin with the rich aroma and warmth. Papa, thankfully, had chopped enough firewood to keep the fire stoked for the next few days. At least until the snow stopped. She hoped.

Maris was in their mother's favorite chair, humming a low tune and tending to the mending. Something she had groused about earlier that day. But with the snow piling up, there wasn't much else to do. Papa was in his chair across from Maris reading an old book with a blue tattered cover. He loved his forgotten lore books as much as Maris loved to complain.

As Serena slowly stirred the stew, dark thoughts clouded her mind. She wished she could run away from this life of poverty. She wished she could provide a better life for her, her sister and Papa. She wished...

Her thoughts trailed away.

She wished.

She stole a glance at Papa who seemed content enough to read and stoke the fire when necessary. And Maris with her needle and thread patching a hole in her cloak.

A restless feeling pounded through Serena. She could not be cooped up in this cabin any longer. She dropped the spoon and swept off the apron that was her mother's and then padded to the front door. She pulled her cloak off the peg and wrapped it around her shoulders, which caught her father's attention.

"Where are you going?" Papa asked.

"I'm taking the pelts into town to trade before we run out of food," she replied, pulling the hood up.

"In this weather?" He sounded incredulous. "You'll catch your death."

"I'll take the horse. It will be easier and faster in this snow," she said.

Papa set aside his book and rose from the chair. "I don't think you should, Serena. The weather is dreadful, and the snow is still coming down."

"Would you rather starve?" Her tone was sharper than she intended. She heaved a sigh, softening her words. "We are nearly out of flour and sugar and low on tea. If I don't go—"

"I'll go instead." He started for his bedroom, his stocking feet silent on the wood floor. "Let me fetch my cloak and boots."

"Papa, no." She huffed her annoyance. She did not want to be trapped in this cabin another moment. "You've only just recovered from your illness. Besides, I know how to negotiate. You taught me, after all."

Plus, it would give her an opportunity to see what the gossip mills were churning about her father's miraculous recovery. And perhaps do some damage control.

"Are you certain you're up to it?" Concern gleamed in his eyes.

"Oh, let her go, Papa. She clearly has a bad case of cabin fever," her sister snarked. "She doesn't want to be trapped in here with us."

Serena bit off the acid retort she had ready and instead turned to heft up the pelts she'd claimed over the summer and early autumn. The heady scent of animal musk wafted to her nose.

"If you're certain..." he said, his voice tentative.

"I'll be back soon. Maris, keep an eye on the stew, will you? I'll not have it burn and go to waste."

She huffed.

"She will," Papa said, his voice sharp.

Which made Serena's gaze snap in his direction. His eyes were hard as he peered at Maris, his arms folded across his chest. It had been a while since he sounded so...fatherly.

"Yes, Papa," Maris said, dropping her gaze back to her mending.

"Be safe, my girl," he said, giving her a nod of farewell.

"I will."

Serena was out the door and around the back of the house to their one-stall stable. But it was difficult to walk in the deep snow. Taking the horse was the right decision.

Her father was once a farrier, but when the illness took their mother and then him, he was no longer able to work. They were luckier than most, though, as they managed to keep one horse for those days when she needed to travel swiftly into the village square. She was grateful for the mare, who snorted her greeting, the breath pluming like steam in the cold air.

"Hello, old girl," she greeted, her voice soft.

After securing the pelts on the back of the horse, she mounted and was away. It was slow going with the horse picking her way through the thickening snow. The village was quiet. All were inside their own homes, with their own fires burning. Serena wondered what she would find in the village square. Surely, the merchant would be open despite the weather.

As she neared the square, the snow turned to slush where other horses and carts had rambled into town, leaving deep rivets in the ground. Still, she kept the horse slow and steady. Only a few brave souls were in town with ruddy cheeks under thick cloaks and scarves wrapped around their necks to ward off the chill.

At the merchant shop, she tied up the horse and hefted the pelts off the back. The door chimed her arrival. Once inside, she stamped her boots leaving behind snow drops. Mr. Brightwood stood at the counter placing an order with the merchant, Mr. Fullhide. They both looked her way as she paused in the door. Mr. Brightwood's dark brows winged upward while Mr. Fullhide's face fell into an unwelcome expression.

But Serena did not let that sway her. "Oh, Mr. Brightwood, hello. How is your ankle faring? Better?"

"Yes, thanks." He turned back to the merchant and picked up a large package wrapped in brown paper. "You'll put this on my account, Gerald?"

"Of course." He gave a nod.

Mr. Brightwood turned from the counter and paused next to her as he passed by. "I hope your father is doing well, miss. His recovery is truly a miracle."

There was a sharp edge to his tone. One she didn't like. But she plastered on a smile, anyway. "I agree it is. My sister and I are thankful he's better."

"Hmm," was all he said as he cut another glance back to Gerald Fullhide.

Then he was out the door. Serena approached the counter, releasing the pelts with a sigh. Her arms were shaking from the exertion. "Good afternoon, Mr. Fullhide. I've come to trade."

He lifted a brow. Mr. Fullhide had been the village merchant since before she could remember. He was a grizzled old man, tall and reedy, with a face hosting a map of wrinkles and eyes that peered through old spectacles that had seen better days. The lenses were scratched, and it was a wonder he was able to see out of them at all. His thin gray hair stuck up around his head in spikes.

"I see. That all you got?"

"Yes." Coming here didn't seem like the best idea. Her nerves rattled.

His gnarled hands rifled through the pelts, looking at them each with a critical eye. "How was it your father made such a recovery?" he asked, clearly more interested in the local gossip than the furs.

"Oh," she breathed. "A tonic." It was as close to the truth as she was willing to get.

His icy gaze lifted as though he didn't believe her, his eyes clouded behind the old lenses. "I heard it was a witch's brew."

"What?" The word sailed out of her before she stopped it. Then she shook her head. "No. Of course not. Wherever did you hear that?"

"Dr. Graves says he didn't treat him," he said.

Ah, so, since the old physician didn't care for her father, then it could be nothing other than a magic concoction. How preposterous. Though, telling him she got the elixir from the stranger at the Well of Wishes seemed preposterous. And what could she say to that? The truth was that the doctor *didn't* treat her father. But if she told Fullhide the truth, he wouldn't believe her, anyway.

"Mrs. Cartweaver said she saw faded tracks leading up to the old mountain a few mornings ago. Know anything about that?" One eye squinted, as though he was trying to pull the truth out of her by glaring.

Curses. She'd left tracks in the snow on her return trip from speaking to the stranger. She'd hoped it would have gone unnoticed, but the slow falling snow didn't cover her footsteps. And Mrs. Cartweaver was the village busybody, anyway.

"Mr. Fullhide, I'm sure I don't know what that means. Now, about the furs—"

"Mrs. Cartweaver said she saw someone coming from the mountain. With a lantern."

Serena forced a laugh. She clenched her jaw. Stars above. What was the old bat doing peering out her window at that time, anyway?

"And?"

"Was it you?" His question was harsh and direct.

She forced herself to remain calm. "What if it was? Am I not allowed to have an early morning stroll?"

"In the cold while it's snowing?" His brow lifted higher.

"The furs, Mr. Fullhide," she said, tersely, trying desperately to get him back on track.

But he continued to peer at her with suspicion.

She didn't owe him an explanation. She didn't owe anyone an explanation. It was difficult to squelch the rumor mill, though.

"They're good enough. I'm sure I can use them." He counted them again. "Legend says the old wishing well is up there. Or used to be." Then he lifted his gaze and peered at her over the tops of his spectacles.

"Is it? I wouldn't know."

Her gut clenched. What was he getting at? Was he trying to find out of she'd gone up there, made a wish and...it came true? If she told him that, then it would spread like wildfire through the village and then the stranger...

The stranger would have no peace.

I pay, too.

This was getting out of hand.

"What do you want for the furs?" he asked.

Relief sputtered through her. They were getting back to the business at hand. "I need the usual. Flour, sugar, tea. A bit of dried meat if you have it."

He packed up her requests adding them to a large brown paper bag and sliding it across the counter to her.

"Thank you, Mr. Fullhide," she said, taking the bag.

"I heard the town folks talking about King Leonidas," Fullhide said, lowering his voice as though the rafters themselves might listen.

That caught her attention. She quirked a brow. "Oh?"

"There's tell he might visit our village."

"Why would he come here?" she asked, truly unnerved by the notion of royalty coming to their poor village.

"Word of your father's recovery—and your generosity with paying the taxman—has reached his ears."

Oh, dear. This wasn't good.

"Has it?" She tried to keep her voice even and steady.

"Mm-hm," Mr. Fullhide said, his gaze piercing her. It was clear there was an unasked question or perhaps an accusation ready to fly off his tongue.

The door chime sounded followed by the stomping of boots on the doormat. "Ah, Fullhide. It's a grand afternoon out there, eh?" The man belly-laughed at that.

Walter Ironroot stomped up to the counter, giving her nothing more than a head nod in greeting. That was all Serena needed to scurry out of the merchant's shop, her heart in her throat.

If the king was coming here, because he'd heard of the things she'd done...the *wishes* she'd made...well, she wasn't sure what was going to happen to her and her family.

Dread pooled in her stomach as she climbed into the saddle and headed for home.

CHAPTER 8

S erena was on edge the moment she returned home and throughout the rest of the evening. She was grateful, though, she had chores to keep her busy while she thought about everything Mr. Fullhide said to her in his shop. He practically accused her of running up to the mountain to the Well of Wishes.

Which she had, but it was still unnerving. She didn't want him to know.

She didn't want *anyone* to know.

Maris chattered away about nothing while they ate their rabbit stew and fresh bread. Papa was quiet through the meal as he listened to her sister make useless conversation.

It grated on Serena's nerves.

But she remained silent. Commenting appropriately when necessary. When at last the meal was over—their only one of the day—she picked up the wooden bowls and busied herself in the kitchen cleaning up. Papa wandered in.

"Do you need help?" he asked.

"I'm good here." She managed a smile, her hands in the warm soapy water. She'd boiled a pot of water to warm it and wash the dishes.

He lingered, hesitation pouring off him as though he had something else to say.

"Did you finish your book?" she asked, trying to make small talk and perhaps find out why he continued to stand there looking at her with an unreadable expression.

"No, no yet."

"Oh, which one is it?" She rinsed a bowl and set it aside to dry, then started washing another one.

"One of the old lore books. You know the one about wishes?"

Her heart climbed its way to her throat. "I can't recall."

"The one about the three wishes and the price the wisher pays for them being granted," he said.

She paused her washing to look at him over her shoulder. He gave her a weak smile. "Merely an old folktale, that's all."

But she wondered why he brought it up. Seemed like he was trying to tell her something. Or perhaps get her to reveal some bit of information.

Yes, Papa. I found the Well of Wishes because I needed to pay the taxman. Because without the gold, we would be homeless, starving, and cast out into the cold and you would have died.

The words flickered through her mind, but she didn't say them.

"What news from the village square?"

Ah, so there it was. He was interested in the town gossip. "The usual. Mr. Fullhide was his normal crusty self." She forced a laugh at that.

She dare not tell him about the king's visit. There was no need to add more stress to their already tension-filled cabin.

"I traded the pelts for flour, a pound of sugar, tea, and some dried meat. That should help us get through the winter," she added.

"Very good, Serena." He left the kitchen, sounding a bit forlorn. As though he wanted to say more, but was unsure what.

Serena heaved a sigh as she finished the dishes.

She should not be thinking of the stranger at the Well of Wishes, but he had been at the forefront of her mind since her return from the merchant. Mr. Fullhide insinuated that he knew about the well—and possibly others in the village—and she worried if that was the case, others would climb the mountain and find their way to the stranger.

And it would be her fault.

She laid in her bed staring at the ceiling wondering what to do. Return to the well? Tell him what she knew? Warn him the king might be visiting?

What would that accomplish?

Nothing, that's what.

But she couldn't put it out of her mind.

Maris snoozed away. Nothing disturbed her or worried her mind. In a fit of agitation, Serena flung off the blankets and rose. She grabbed her dressing gown from the end of the bed and wrapped it around her, then crept out of her room.

The fire had burned down to nothing more than glowing orange and red embers. Papa was not in his chair, which likely meant he'd made his way to bed. She was relieved. He needed his rest, despite his renewed strength.

But he'd left his book behind. It was open and upside down in the chair.

Curious, she picked it up and scanned the page. The story was called *Three Wishes*, and it was about a poor man who was granted three wishes by a fairy but warned that all wishes come at a price. The man's wife insisted on waiting to make the best wishes, but he did not and ended up squandering away two of the wishes on frivolous things. This angered his wife and, in a fit of rage, he wished her away, which he immediately regretted. He begged the fairy for another wish to bring her back. The fairy told him if he could find her true name, he may have one more final wish to return his wife.

Serena stopped reading, her head snapping up as an idea formed. She clutched the book so tight, her hands cramped.

"Find the fairy's true name," she muttered.

What was it the stranger said to her?

A name is a lock, and the tongue that speaks it is the key.

"Stars above. That's it."

She placed her father's book back in his chair, then hurried to her room. Maris slept on while Serena quickly dressed.

This was madness.

She could not believe she was considering returning to the mountain. It was a risk, she knew, but one she was willing to take. If she returned to the Well of Wishes, she could ask the stranger that if speaking his true name would release him from his bondage.

That stopped her. She froze, her boots in her hand as she stared into the murky darkness.

What was she doing? Why did she care? This stranger meant nothing to her.

But something about the way he looked at her tugged at her heart. That desolate expression in his green-blue eyes sent a pang right through her. He had not asked for help. Perhaps he didn't need or want it. Perhaps he was content to be bound to the Well of Wishes.

But what if she could help him? What if she could find his true name? Would that, then, release him?

I pay, too.

She could warn him the villagers suspected he was there. She could tell him the king was coming to pay the village a visit.

And she would not make another wish, no matter how tempted.

She pulled on her cloak, wrapping it tight around her, then tiptoed to the front door. She snagged the lantern off the floor, put on her boots, and slipped into the brisk night.

The climb was cold and long, but she was determined to make her way to the Well of Wishes.

The stranger stood next to the well, as though waiting for her. His eyes glinted with expectation, his lips in a firm, straight line. The wind flapped at the edges of his cloak. He did not look pleased to see her.

She held up her lantern to get a good look at this face. Her breath caught. He was handsome in an otherworldly sort of way. The hood was up, as it always was, shadowing most of his face. But his eyes...they pierced right through her.

"Again you come." His voice strained. Displeasure lined his features. "Why?"

"I—" She pressed her lips together, unsure what to say. "There is gossip in the village."

He lifted a brow, curiosity replacing disdain as it flickered across his handsome features. "What is this gossip?"

"They are calling my father's return to health a miracle."

"Is that not what you wished for? A miracle?"

"Yes, but—"

"Then why does that vex you, Serena?"

She sucked in a breath, expelled it. Her breath crystalized in the air. "I'm worried that...the villagers suspect something."

"I see," he said. "Have they branded you a witch yet? Do they wish to convict you for a crime you have not committed? Is that why you are here?"

"No!" she gasped. Though it occurred to her Fullhide asked if it was a witch's brew she gave Papa. "It's not that. It's—"

He lifted a brow and stepped closer to her. As he did, she noticed his height. He was at least a head taller than her, which made her tip her head back to look up at him. A fluttering erupted in her chest as her breath pooled in her throat. His gaze searched her face, then his features softened.

"You are frightened."

"I think the villagers suspect the Well is still here."

"It *is* still here."

"But I mean...the villagers don't *know* that for sure. They think it's nothing more than folklore. I thought it was, too, until that day I—"

She broke off, thinking of that desperately frigid night as she climbed the mountain with the last shred of hope. And then there he was. But he did not appear immediately.

"You sought the Well of Wishes," he finished for her.

She nodded. Her gut burned as she peered at him, trying to find the words to tell him...to ask him...to warn him.

His shoulders dropped, and he stepped back toward the Well. "You fear for my safety."

"Yes," she replied.

"That's why you came?"

The lantern glinted in his eyes as he peered at her. She saw emotion there she did not understand. Was he...glad she came? Or annoyed?

"I thought I should warn you."

His puffed breath fogged before him as he sagged against the edge of the well, looking off into the distance toward the village. "I confess you are the first person I've seen in a long time. The first person who dared climb the mountain. Who dared find the Well." He tipped his head to one side. "How did you know about it?"

She thought of her father's book collection.

"There are...old tales that speak of a magical wishing well that can grant wishes. I read it in a storybook long ago."

He scoffed. "A bedtime story, no doubt. Those are for children."

"But it's real. *You* are real." She moved toward him and he flinched, as though he did not want her to get so close. "Do you not wish to be released of your burden?"

He narrowed his gaze at her. "What are you playing at, Serena?"

"N-nothing. It's—I thought...that..." Her words trailed away. She took a step back, clutching the lantern tighter in her hand. It swung at her side, sending a garish slashing of light across the leaf-cluttered ground.

"You thought to break my curse?" He gave a humorless laugh. "Many have tried. None have succeeded."

She lifted her chin a little higher. "What if I did?"

This time, he laughed out loud. "You may try, I suppose. But I have my doubts you will succeed."

"You know how to break it, don't you?" she asked, determination edging through her.

He said nothing as he pressed his lips together into a thin line.

In desperation, she said, "If I guess your true name, will it free you?"

The stranger froze. He was so still, he looked as though he'd turned to stone. He stared at her out of those green-blue eyes that now glinted with something she could not understand. Fear? Remorse? Hope? She wasn't sure.

"Where did you hear that?"

"I read it in a book. And...something you said. That a name is a lock and the tongue that speaks it is the key."

His jaw clenched, the muscles ticking along the edge, though he said nothing.

"Is that it?" she pressed.

"Why do you wish to help me?" he demanded, then, his voice hard and cold. "I am nothing to you."

"Because you ..." Her breath hitched as she glanced down at her snow-crusted boots. "You gave me hope when I had none."

When she looked up again, his eyes searched her face, sharp as glass, wanting to believe her. But then he turned away, shoulders bowed beneath an invisible weight.

"Hope is dangerous, Serena Windriver," he murmured. "It will betray you in the end."

She wanted to argue. But the words lodged in her throat. And so she stood in silence, his warning echoing in her ears and her heart pounding like a drum. His cloak snapped in the wind, his face hidden once more in shadow.

"Go home, Serena," he said softly. "Before the Well decides your fate, too."

Lantern trembling in her hand, she stumbled back a step as her throat tightened. Tears threatened. She should leave. She should run. But all she could think was that somewhere behind those green-blue eyes, he was begging her to stay.

"But, I—"

"Go," he said again, his tone sharp.

As she stumbled away into the snow, she wondered if he was right—if hope was already the most dangerous wish of all.

Chapter 9

The stranger watched the girl hurry down the mountain and disappear out of sight. He turned away and leaned against the stone, breath catching in his throat. The Well shimmered, magic curling like glittering smoke beneath the surface, ready and waiting for him to grant her wish. Hungry for it.

But she did not make a wish.

No, instead, she came to him and asked how to release him from his captivity. His curse.

Why? Why would she want to do such a thing?

You gave me hope.

Oh, *Gods*, why did she have to say that? Why did she have to look at him with those beautiful eyes full of compassion and empathy? Why did her words tug at his heart when he thought his heart was long since gone?

He regretted his words—that a name is a lock and the tongue that speaks it is the key. He should have guarded his thoughts. But he didn't and now...now the girl returned seeking more answers. Seeking truth.

Every time she came back, the fragments of his memory pieced together. Every time she returned, a little light returned to his world. Every time she returned, warmth glowed in his broken heart.

Every single time.

That first moment when he met her, something shifted deep inside him. He felt it, as real as he felt his breath expand in his lungs. The cold pierced him, making him shiver. For the first time in ages, he felt *alive*.

That first day, her face was lined with desperation. She did not beg as others had in the past. She simply made the wish, her voice strong and sure as she said the words. There was no power in this realm that could refuse her. He was compelled to grant her wish as he was compelled to remove the memory of her mother.

And he hated himself for that.

His self-loathing grew when she returned a second time to ask him to save her father and he took away her memory of her father's love.

He was grateful she didn't make a third wish. Another piece of him died as he turned her away and made a desperate, silent plea for her to never return.

The girl returns. And yet she does not wish.

The stranger's head snapped up. The Well had not spoken in years.

Perhaps I shall send for her. A low, deep chuckle from the Well.

"Leave her be," he snapped, his breath crystallizing in the air around him. "She is nothing to you."

But she is something to YOU, Weaver of Wishes.

His eyes closed as he leaned on the stone edge. He dropped his head and murmured, "Please."

Oh, how the mighty have fallen.

He ignored the voice, refusing to acknowledge the barb. Yes, he was once a Fae Prince of the Seelie Court. Until—

No. He shoved that away, pushing the memories back down into the dark recesses of his mind.

You keep her memories close to you, do you not? The Well requires them and yet you have not deposited the price she paid. The price you took.

His stomach knotted. He hadn't deposited her memory. Hadn't given the Well its price. He had refused. And in his moments when he was the loneliest, when the realm had abandoned him once again and the woods were cold and silent, he conjured the one of her mother making a flower wreath and placing it on her head. Serena's laughter was warm and infectious. Her smile, beautiful and bright. Her joy, palpable.

You keep them because they remind you of HER. Another disembodied laugh.

"They do," he admitted. And, gods, he hated that admission, too.

Fool.

"No," he snapped. His gut churned acid. Then, slumping to the ground, he put his face in his gloved hands. "Yes. I am a fool. Worse than that."

Serena's dazzling smile reminded him of the mortal girl he once loved. But not just her smile. Her kindness. Her bravery. Her selflessness. In truth, he could not recall his lover's face or the sound of her voice or the way her hair smelled. Perhaps he *was* foolish to project those feelings onto Serena.

But somewhere deep within him, he was certain it was more than that. It was a growing feeling.

Thinking of the girl he once loved was like an arrow piercing his heart. Painful. So painful. All he wanted to do was help her and so, he did. He gave freely, which broke the laws of Fae magic—the laws that say all magical things must be bartered and all power must be earned. Now, he was nothing more than a vessel through which all wishes must be spun.

He had become the weaver—neither prince nor shadow, forever trapped in the mortal realm collecting payment from all who wished.

She will return. And when she does, the price will be high. Are you prepared, weaver, to take it?

His jaw clenched so tight, his teeth ached. Refusing was not an option. The Well knew that as he did.

If she returned, the Well would demand more. A darker memory or, perhaps, even her name. And he—he would take it. Because he always did.

"Yes," he faintly said, the word ice.

He sent up his own fervent wish.

Stay away, Serena. Do not return. Not because I do not wish it...but because if you do...I will take something I can never give back.

CHAPTER 10

The Grand Duke arrived with a small company. He made his residence in the village inn located in the square. News of his arrival spread quickly. Papa bustled into the cabin that morning with an armload of firewood and his eyes alight with excitement.

"The Grand Duke is here!" he announced.

Serena turned from the washbasin, a dish still in hand. He wasn't jesting. Maris dropped her needlework and jumped to her feet.

"Truly, Papa?" Excitement tinged her words.

"Whatever could he be doing here?" Serena asked, absently.

The last she heard, it was the king who was planning to visit.

"Oh, Serena, everyone knows the king has a son," Maris said, clapping her hands with glee. "Perhaps the Grand Duke is here to find the prince a bride."

And she hoped, no doubt, that bride would be her. Serena couldn't blame her sister for wanting to get out of here. She, herself, wanted that, too, but she knew it was impossible.

"That only happens in fairy tales," Serena snorted. She waved away the silly thought her sister could be the one to catch the prince's eye.

It earned her a heated glare from Maris. "It could happen," she said with a frown.

Serena ignored her. She doubted the Grand Duke would visit to pick a girl for the prince from their poor village. There were likely better prospects throughout the realm. Most in her village were struggling to survive like they were. Thankfully, their autumn harvest had been plentiful, and Papa was able to keep them in firewood.

"I heard from Mr. Ironroot he's in town asking a lot of questions." Papa stacked the firewood in the log holder by the hearth, then dusted his hands and turned to face her. He folded his arms across his chest.

She did not miss the pointed look he gave her. "What sort of questions?"

"Apparently, word spread to the king about my recovery," he said.

Oh, Gods. That wasn't good. Mr. Fullhide was right, then.

"And..." He added, then paused, "that you paid the taxman for not only us, but another family. Is this true, Serena?"

There was a hard edge to his voice. One she didn't like. Maris snapped her head in her direction. Her eyes were wide with shock.

The day Serena returned from the Well of Wishes with the satchel full of gold, she had told no one where she got it. Not even Maris. She simply handed over the gold to the taxman and then put it out of her mind.

But someone noticed and someone talked. She cursed herself for being so foolish. Her act of generosity garnered royal attention. Attention she and her family could not afford.

It wasn't about the taxman, either. It was about the healing elixir. Dr. Graves had mentioned he hadn't treated Papa, and someone told Mr. Fullhide.

She clenched her hand into a fist.

She said, "It is true."

Papa's face drained of color as he stared at her in stunned silence. "Serena—how—?"

"Please do not ask me to explain," she snapped.

She whirled away and busied herself washing dishes once again.

"Did you...where did you get the gold, Serena?" Papa asked.

He sounded hurt, distressed, and worried.

How could she tell him the truth? If she did, she'd reveal the Well of Wishes and...the stranger. And Maris...well, she couldn't be trusted. Her sister would tell anyone and everyone who would listen. Her sister would brag about their imagined wealth and then demand Serena share it with her.

Papa, on the other hand...she'd thought a million times about telling him. But she stopped herself because she'd feared he would not understand.

"Did you...steal it, Serena?"

The accusation hit her like a punch in the gut. She dropped the bowl she was washing into the hot soapy water and spun to face him.

"No! I would never do such a thing."

"Then where did you get it?" His expression was tight, on edge.

Maris gaped, her gaze swinging between the two of them.

Serena pressed her lips together into a tight line. "I-I..." She halted, sucked in a breath, and then lied. "I sold a stack of animal pelts to Mr. Fullhide."

Air whooshed out of Papa as he dropped his arms, relieved. But then, his expression creased with question. "And the elixir?"

She swallowed hard, her mouth turning to ash. "Papa, you know I have some experience with herbs. I made it myself."

He stared at her a long, questioning moment as he contemplated this.

"But you left that night," Maris piped up. "You were gone for hours when you came back with the elixir."

Stars above. Why couldn't Maris let it go?

"I think you're mistaken," Serena said, her voice tight.

"No, I'm not. I remember you—"

"That's enough, Maris," she snapped.

"But—"

"Maris," Papa said, his voice soft. "It's all right, little dove. Serena has her secrets. Let her keep them."

But he gave her a warning glance. That she was not to keep her secrets from *him*.

Maris stuck out her lower lip in a spectacular pout as she stomped away to their room and slammed the door. Serena sighed and turned back to the sink to resume washing.

"I don't know why you lied, Serena, but I hope it's for a good reason."

She gripped the edge of the sink, knuckles white. One more lie, layered on top of the last. It wouldn't hold forever. And when it shattered, so would she.

"Don't ask me to explain, Papa. I cannot," she said sharply.

His brow furrowed. "I'll accept that. For now."

He left the room. Alone again, she faced the suds and the silence—and the weight of every secret she wasn't strong enough to speak aloud.

Later that day after their evening meal, they were enjoying amicable silence by the crackling fire. Papa with his book. Maris with her needlework. Serena trying to focus on her own sewing to repair a hole in her cloak. But her thoughts drifted back to the stranger and the way he rebuffed her. Why did it bother her so?

Hope is dangerous, Serena Windriver.

Perhaps he'd given up hope long ago he would be freed from his duties at the Well of Wishes. Why did she care so much?

Was it because of the way he looked at her when she arrived that last time with the offer to release him?

Many have tried. None have succeeded.

And why was she so determined to succeed?

"Serena, you all right?" Papa asked.

She realized she was holding the needle and thread and staring into space. She blinked to clear the thoughts from her head and focused on her father. She managed a smile.

"Lost in thought."

Maris cut her a sideways glance before returning to her own sewing. Her father returned to his book. Serena focused on the tattered cover and the faded gold embossed lettering of the title. *Folklore and Fairy Tales.*

Idly, she wondered if there was something in that book to help her break the stranger's curse.

She shoved the thought away as she stuck the needle into the fabric of her cloak. There were no answers in a book about fairy tales that could help her. A knock sounded on the cabin door. Immediately, Serena's heart clawed its way to her throat. Papa snapped his book closed and rose to answer it while Maris continued her sewing by the fire.

The Grand Duke stood on the other side of the door. Tall and lean, snow dotted the shoulders of his thick fur-lined cloak which was draped like a mantle of command. His black hair was slicked back from his high forehead. No hair was out of place. Steel-gray eyes peered out of an angular face with high cheekbones giving the air of aristocracy. A thin mouth gave the impression he seldom smiled.

"Your grace." Her father bowed. "You honor us with your visit."

Maris dropped her needlework and shot to her feet, her eyes alight with surprise. Serena, her breathing shallow, slowly rose and placed her cloak in the seat of her chair.

"Master Windriver, is it?"

"Yes, your grace." He stepped aside. "Please come in out of the cold. Would you like tea?"

He ordered his guards to wait outside in the snow as he stepped into their small cabin. His posture was impeccable, his stance authoritative. He pulled off his cloak with a flourish, the snow falling to the floor around him and immediately melting. He handed off the cloak to Papa with practiced precision as her father closed the door, then hung up the cloak.

He removed his gloves, his sharp assessing gaze taking in the confines of their small cabin. It was clear the man missed nothing.

"Tea, yes."

"I'll fetch it," Serena said, glad to escape the tiny living room. The air had become oppressive.

"My daughter, Serena," Papa said. "And my youngest, Maris."

The Grand Duke nodded, the only acknowledgement. "There's talk in the village about your family."

With shaking hands, Serena prepared the tea, thankful the kettle was still on and warm. She poured it into the porcelain teapot that was her mother's, then arranged four cups, the sugar bowl, and the creamer.

"Folks like to talk, your grace. I'm afraid there's not much else to do during winter." There was a smile in her father's voice as he tried to disarm him.

But the Grand Duke was not to be disarmed. His expression remained hard and unrelenting. "Nevertheless, word made it to his majesty, the king. That's why I'm here. That taxman reports you paid in full. Curious, when your family is said to have so little."

He punctuated that with another glance around the cabin. No doubt noticing their worn and scuffed furniture.

Serena carried the tray into the living room as Papa offered the Grand Duke his chair. His booted feet left puddles of melted snow across the floor. When he sat, his flinty gaze moved from Maris to her.

She placed the tray on the low table between the chairs. He watched with feigned interest as she poured the tea then handed him the cup.

"Cream or sugar, your grace?" she asked.

He waved it away. Then to Papa, he said, "His majesty is keen to know how you were able to pay the taxes not only for yourself but for the other family."

Tense silence stretched. Serena busied herself with pouring another cup and handed it to Maris with a warning look. She prayed to the stars above her sister remained mute. Maris took the cup, holding it between shaking hands.

"A bountiful harvest, your grace," Papa said. "And my daughter is a fine huntress. She traded pelts for the gold."

"Is that so?" He peered at her over the edge of the cup, the steam rising from the tawny liquid.

Serena poured more tea and handed it to Papa. He waved it away. She plastered on a smile. "Indeed, it is."

"You're telling me you sold animal skins to raise enough money?"

"Yes, your grace," Serena said.

His gaze turned to her father then. "And your recovery, Master Windriver. Dr. Graves says it was a miracle, that even the best healers from the realm could not heal you. And yet, you stand before me. Hearty and hale."

Papa cleared his throat and clasped his hands behind his back. But Serena saw them shaking before he did so. He was nervous.

So was she.

She cast a glance to her sister, who remained pale faced, wide eyed, and mute. Thank the stars.

"An elixir, your grace," she said, stepping forward. "I am good with herbs and the like."

A dark brow lifted as he pinned her with his cold stare. "You cured him?"

"Yes." It was not so far from the truth, but her voice shook a little with her response.

"Rather the miracle worker, aren't you, Mistress Serena?" he said, snidely.

Silence stretched as he peered at her, then took a sip of tea. He leaned forward and deposited the cup on the tray, then rose. His height was imposing. His gaze unflinching. And Serena suspected he saw through her. The only sound was that of the thudding of her heart in her ears.

The Grand Duke paused so close to her, she smelled horse and leather. She lifted her eyes to his and met his gaze.

"A lie is a dangerous thing, Mistress Serena. Not because of the telling, but because of the keeping. They weigh heavier than gold."

Hot fear pulsed through her as the man stepped toward the door and removed his cloak. He pulled it on around his narrow shoulders.

"I take my leave." But his cold eyes landed on her once more. "The king is interested in miracles, Mistress Serena. Expect me again."

And then, he whisked open the door and was gone.

CHAPTER 11

That night, Serena found it difficult to sleep. Maris wasn't speaking to her, even when she tried to apologize for her snarky comment.

With her mother's shawl wrapped around her shoulders, she curled in the chair by the fire. When the flames got too low, she placed another log on it. She grappled with everything that had happened. The stranger at the Well of Wishes. Lying to Papa. Lying to the Grand Duke. His veiled threat that he would be back. She could not stop playing his last words over and over in her head.

The king is interested in miracles, Mistress Serena. Expect me again.

He was going to return with the king in tow. And when he did...then what? What miracle did he expect from her? Without knowing, she could not go back to the Well of Wishes to ask for—

She stopped that thought before it fully formed. No, she would not return. She would not risk more than she already had. She'd lost two precious things to her—even if they were things she did not remember. She could not afford to lose more.

But the king—

Her stomach was coiled into a tight knot as she clutched her elbows, her eyes fixed on the flickering flames in the hearth.

Papa's bedroom door opened, and he shuffled out. He halted there, his eyes dark orbs in the shadows. He was surprised to see her.

"Couldn't sleep?" he asked.

"No. You?" she replied.

"No. I suppose insomnia is better with company."

Heaving a heavy sigh and clutching a book under his arm, he lowered himself into his favorite chair across from her. The book rested in his lap as he gazed at her from across the fire, the yellow light flickering across his haggard features.

She had done that to him. She had made him weary and suspicious. But now, she was so far in, how could she tell him the truth? The lies and secrets were her burden to bear.

They sat in silence for a time. His gaze drifted to the fire, his hand clutching the well-worn book. Outside, the wind howled low, swishing through what leaves were left on the trees and clacking the branches together. It was a quiet night. Too quiet.

"You carry a heavy burden, daughter," he said at last breaking into the silence. "Tell me what it is."

"Papa..." Her voice drifted.

"Secrets are heavy things, Serena. Too heavy to carry alone."

This she understood, because she had been carrying the secret of the stranger close to her since the moment she stepped off the mountain with a satchel full of gold.

His worried gaze landed on her again. "Tell me. Before it eats you alive."

She clutched the shawl tighter around her frame. She took a deep, cleansing breath to steady her heart. "Do you recall the old folklore about the Well of Wishes?"

Papa stiffened and clutched his book tighter. "I do."

Serena's mouth went dry, but she forced herself to forge onward. "Most folks think it is nothing more than a myth. That it doesn't exist, but I…" She swallowed hard. "I found it. I went there."

His eyes widened as he stared at her in shock. "Serena—"

"I didn't know what else to do, you see," she rushed on. "The taxes, your illness…I-I couldn't let you die. I couldn't let us be thrown out of our home."

His shoulders sagged, as though in defeat. "Gods, girl. You made a bargain."

"I had to. It was the only way—"

"Serena." He scraped a hand down his face, leaving a bloodless trail she could see in the flickering light. "Gods, do you know what you've done? The Well always takes more than it gives. You mustn't go back. You *must never* go back. Promise me."

"Papa—"

"Promise, Serena." Worry lines creased his forehead. He looked as though he'd aged ten years hearing her confession.

And she hated herself for that. She hated what she had done, but she knew it was the only way to keep a roof over their head and save her father.

She wanted to promise and keep it. But the stranger's green-blue eyes and face etched in sorrow with a bit of hope haunted her. His voice, his sorrow, his curse. Deep down she was certain she would find a way to free him from his horrible burden. If only she could find his true name. Her gaze flicked to the book clutched in Papa's hand.

"Will you promise?" he asked.

As emotion clotted her throat and tears threatened, she nodded. And even as she promised, she knew she would not keep it.

He blew out a breath. "I'm glad you told me."

"What will we do about the Grand Duke and the king?" she asked, then, worried about the coming days.

He gave her a faint smile. "We will think of something."

"But—"

"Shh. There's nothing to be done about it this night."

His tone was gentle, reminding her of days long past when she was a girl and he was larger than life. Now, he was weaker, older. Still her Papa, but different. Aged.

"You have dark circles under your eyes. Go rest," he said.

She didn't want to face her sister in the morning. Her hands cramped, and she realized she clutched the shawl far too tight.

"I will think of some way to deal with the king and the Grand Duke," he said at last.

There was that self-loathing again. She had put this burden on him, and it shouldn't be his. But she uncurled her legs from underneath her and rose with a nod. She kissed his cheek.

"Good night, Papa."

She turned toward her room, Papa's warning echoing in her chest. *You must never go back.* But in her heart, she knew she already would.

Days later, the king arrived in the village with much fanfare. His entourage was so large, it coiled like a snake throughout the village. At least, that's what it looked like to Serena.

Snow fell in earnest, blanketing the rooftops and muffling the world as if the village itself held its breath. The horses churned the road into gray slush as they clopped through the square. All the villagers were out to watch the processional. All were bundled in their cloaks, hoods pulled tight around their heads. Even Serena, Papa, and Maris stood outside in the falling snow, their breath fogging in front of them as the king arrived in their small village of Stonemere.

Despite the cold and her threadbare gloves, Serena's palms broke into a hot sweat. Her nerves jangled as the King's Guard, riding two by two, passed. The carriage was in the center flanked by more guards. Even more were behind it. The heraldry of the king—flags in gold and plum with his sigil of a roaring gold lion—flapped in the chilled wind at the front of the line.

The line slowed and came to a halt. The carriage only a few steps from their modest cottage, which made her heart ram in her throat.

"They're stopping here?" Maris said in a roughened whisper.

Serena glanced at Papa, whose eyes were fixed on the carriage, his brow creased with worry. He said nothing as he looked her way, and she saw the fear there. And it was her fault. She alone had put them in this position.

They had not discussed what would happen should the king turn up on their doorstep. Now, it was too late for that.

Maris shivered, pulling her cloak tighter as she peered at the ornate carriage with unabashed awe. Serena turned her gaze forward and tried to steel her nerves, but her heart continued to pound like a drum.

A footman was at the door in an instant, pulling it open and standing aside, waiting for his majesty to exit.

A moment later, he stepped down from the carriage, his labored breath wheezing in and out followed by a watery cough.

Serena did not get a good look at him as she curtsied with the rest of the villagers, bowing her head low in respect for the king.

"Ah, so this is Stonemere," he said. The king had a big, booming voice. He did not sound pleased to be there.

"Yes, your majesty," the Grand Duke replied.

Serena peeked to see the man standing next to the king. His thin frame was wrapped in his fine cloak as it was the day he visited them. His steely eyes moved across the villagers.

Then a woman said in a pinched voice full of disdain, "What a *wretched* place."

"My dear, please try to refrain yourself," the king chastised. Then to the villagers, "Rise, please."

Serena lifted her head as did Papa and Maris. They stood side by side, snow dotting their shoulders and heads. She got her first look at King Leonidas.

He was a short, portly man wearing the finest clothes. His fur-lined cloak was pulled tight around his thick frame. His head was uncovered. His cheeks red from the cold. His eyes, bright blue and flicking from one person to the next, paused on her. Then back to her father. The wind tousled his thinning hair, making it stick up from his head. He emitted another cough, low and deep in his chest.

Next to him, the queen. Her pinched expression was full of contempt as she looked down her nose at each and every one of them. She, too, wore a fur-lined cloak, but her hood was drawn up to cover her head. She clutched it tight with a gloved hand that was be-ringed, the jewels glinting in the late afternoon light. She clearly looked as though she wished to be anywhere but there.

The village mayor bustled up, his breath see-sawing in and out as he hurried to greet the king. He bowed low.

"Your majesties, you honor our humble village with your presence. I'm Mayor Whitesmith. I welcome you both to Stonemere."

The queen glanced at the mayor but said nothing. The king clapped the man on the back in a good-natured sign, as though they were long-lost chums.

"I understand this is the village of miracles," the king said.

Mayor Whitesmith did not hide his confusion. Or perhaps it was merely his way of refusing to acknowledge the gossip.

"Miracles, sire?"

"Yes, yes." Then the king's gaze moved across the three of them. Then he looked at the Grand Duke, the mayor forgotten. "Lachlan, did you not tell me this was the house?"

He gave a bow of his head. "Indeed, I did, your majesty."

"I'm sure that's nothing more than local gossip, your majesty," the mayor said with a weak smile and weaker voice.

But the king ignored the mayor as his gaze swung back to the three of them and stopped on Serena. He stepped closer to her, and she smelled the rich scent of port and cigar smoke wafting off him.

"Mistress Serena?" he asked.

She dipped a low curtsey. "Yes, your majesty."

"His Grace has told me about you and your miracles," he said, then punctuated that with another cough that sounded dreadful. "I wish for your help."

"My help, your majesty?" She tried to keep her voice even and calm.

Next to her, Maris shifted uneasily. Papa placed a hand on her arm to steady her and, hopefully, keep her quiet.

"Your majesty, my daughter is not a healer," Papa said then.

"Ah, so you're the one."

The king moved to stand in front of Papa, giving him a good once over. Papa, to his credit, remained calm and still and his eyes forward.

"But your daughter, Master Windriver, is the one who gave you this mysterious elixir to cure you." Then, he gave his attention to the Grand Duke. "Isn't that what you told me, Lachlan?"

"It is, sire." When he replied, his gaze was fixed solely on Serena.

Her nerves jangled. Fear clawed its way from her gut to her throat, and her mouth had gone dry.

Papa gave a weak smile. "She is indeed the one and is good with herbs, but—"

"Then I wish for her help." He sidestepped back down to halt in front of Serena.

Behind him, the Grand Duke did not bother to hide his smug expression. The queen, next to him, looked on with a mix of curiosity and contempt. The mayor wrung his hands together trying to decide if and how to intervene, his expression pinched with a mixture of fear and worry.

Serena swallowed hard. "How may I help, your majesty?"

"My son is ill, you see. Desperate times, and all that. I should like you to return with us to the palace. Of course, you'll have whatever herbs you need and my staff will be at your disposal."

Serena was stunned into silence. Heat crawled up her neck at the idea of leaving the village to go to the royal palace. "I...don't know what to say, your majesty."

She cut a glance to her father, who stood rooted in place. His face had drained of color. Maris nearly vibrated out of her skin. Either from jealousy or excitement, or perhaps both.

Papa spoke up then.

"Your majesty, it will be a...loss...if my daughter leaves. She keeps the household running and—"

"Yes, yes, Lachland explained all that to me." He waved the thought away as though it didn't matter. Then to her, he added, "The crown will be indebted to you if you succeed in curing my only son. He is, after all, the crown prince."

He left the reward unsaid, but the promise clung to the air.

Maris emitted a strangled gasp that, thankfully, everyone ignored. Papa remained tall and stiff in the cold, his apprehensive gaze remaining on the king, then landed on her. His expression was guarded, as though he understood she dare not refuse. He started to speak, but she gave one quick shake of her head. He pressed his lips together in a thin line.

Refusal would be ruin. Higher taxes, harsher punishments, the village crushed beneath the crown's heel. But acceptance...acceptance meant stepping into a trap. Her mouth was dry. Her throat raw.

Slowly, she turned to the king, dread clawing at her, but her chin lifted all the same.

"I would be honored, your majesty." She dipped a low curtsy.

"Good, then, can we go home now?" the queen asked. She didn't wait for a reply as she stepped back to the carriage, waiting for the door to open and grant her entrance.

The king ignored his wife as he reached for Serena's hand, holding it between his gloved ones. Warmth pressed though her chilled fingers.

"We leave at first light."

Then he released her, climbed into the carriage after his wife and the Grand Duke. Moments later, the entourage was off leaving her with a wickedly pounding heart and the dread coiling low and hot in her belly.

CHAPTER 12

T he sky was pitch black. No moon to light the way. The snow had stopped, but it still blanketed the rooftops, the street, the treetops. Deep ruts were left from the king's carriage.

Serena stood outside the cabin, the cloak pulled tight around her, and the lantern clutched in her hand. Yellow light illuminated the glittering snow.

Cold seeped through her weary bones. The thought of trudging up the mountain was enough to make her turn around and go back inside. Papa slept. Maris slept. Now was her chance.

She had to go.

She had to see *him*. The stranger at the Well of Wishes. He was the only one who could help her now.

A risk. She knew. A risk she was willing to take.

She needed to make one last wish. One that would help her when she was in the palace.

Her breath turned white in front of her as she started down the path. Her booted feet crunched on new-fallen snow. The only thing that kept her going was that when she crested the hilltop, he would be there, and he would help her.

Her legs ached. Even as fear gripped her, hope burned bright and hot within her breast. Hope that the stranger—whose name she still had not found—would grant her one last wish. She didn't care what it cost her.

Or maybe she did. Her life was forfeit either way. If the stranger at the Well of Wishes did not help her, then she would fail when she arrived at the palace. She tried not to think about that. Or the way Maris threw a tantrum about her going. She begged to go with her, but Papa refused to allow it, which was a relief. Serena was not sure Maris would do her any favors. She knew too much.

She saw him before she even made it to the top. The stranger stood stiff, his bright eyes glinted with a hint of fear. The hood hid most of his face, but even so she still saw the map of regret, of sorrow, of pain.

"Why did you return?" he demanded, his voice thick with emotion she did not understand.

He was angry she had returned.

Serena paused to catch her breath, her lungs on fire. "You know why. The king has come and needs me to heal his ailing son."

"The cost is too great, Serena." His mouth turned down into a frown.

"Are you to refuse my wish?" Her tongue was sharp, though she did not intend for it to sound like a demand.

You cannot deny the wisher, weaver.

She sucked in a breath, glancing around the area looking for the owner of the strange voice. "Who was that?"

The stranger stepped forward, his eyes pleading and his voice quiet but shaking. "Please don't make me do this."

There was something in the way he said it that gave her pause. She looked at him and was unnerved. He peered at her with those bright blue eyes that begged her to leave, to return to the village. She closed the gap between them with one step, tipping her head back to look up at him.

Here, in the shadows, his face was nearly concealed by the hood he always wore. His burning gaze met hers and for a moment, she thought she saw something there. Some hint of desire or need. But then that seemed ridiculous, didn't it? He didn't know her. She didn't know him.

And yet...she wanted to find his true name and release him from his bondage.

"Why do you hide beneath the hood?" she whispered and her voice shook.

He said nothing. His jaw clenched, the muscles flexing there. Her free hand moved before her mind told her to stop. She rested it on his cheek. Smooth. Warm.

He flinched and tried to jerk away from her.

"Why?" she repeated.

His gaze bored into hers. And in that moment, something shifted between them. In his eyes, she saw all the lonely years of his life tethered here to this place, where wishes were granted and bargains were made. Without looking away, he reached up and pushed off the hood.

The material fell back, revealing him to her for the first time. And for a moment, she stopped breathing. Her breath pooled in her throat.

Hair pale as moonlight spilled down his back and over his shoulders. It was as if the hood had held it firmly in place. He wore a silver circlet, the intricate knotwork resting against his forehead at a point.

His face was handsome. Perfect cheekbones as though chiseled by the gods themselves. Full lips. A chin that tapered to a point with a dimple in the center.

But the thing that surprised her the most was his ears formed a delicate point.

"You are...Fae." When she said it, the words bloomed in a fog in front of her.

"And you are mortal," he replied. "Please, Serena, do not ask me to grant another wish."

The weaver does not decide, the strange voice said.

She shivered. "Who is that?" she asked, quietly.

"The Well," he replied, as quiet.

Make your wish, Serena Windriver, and pay the price. For all bargains come with a price.

"It knows why I've come, doesn't it?" she asked.

He nodded.

"I-I..." And then she pressed her lips together, unsure. Her heart pounded against her ribs. "You know the price is too high, don't you?"

"The price is always too high," he replied. "But if you must...make your wish and I will grant it for I have no other choice."

He sounded sad when he said it, making her chest ache.

"You care for me. You don't want me to make it."

The stranger turned away to face the Well. He leaned his gloved hands on the edge of the stone and peered down. "I must do my duty."

Duty first.

She swallowed hard. "The king asks me to heal his son. I don't know what ails him. I'm to go with him at first light to the palace."

"The palace?" he echoed. He looked at her over his shoulder, surprise and concern on his face.

"Yes. The Grand Duke...he knows I am a fraud. Please, you must help me. I fear what they'll do to me and my family if I fail." The words spilled out in a heated rush.

A long quiet moment passed as he peered at her. In his eyes she saw pain, and she saw acquiescence. He pulled off his gloves and placed them aside on the edge of the Well. The runes carved into his skin glowed gold. He held them out to her.

"Give me your hands."

Serena dropped the lantern at her feet and reached for him, putting her hands in his. They were warm and soft. The moment their skin touched, it sent a thrill through her and a curious sweeping through her belly. Her breathing was ragged. Her heart was pounding.

The stranger pulled her close, so close barely an inch separated them.

"Make your wish, Serena Windriver. Say the words and it will be granted."

Her throat burned. One wish and she'd save the crown prince. Without it, she'd fail and doom her family. She took a deep breath, expelled it.

"I wish for the power to heal the king's son."

"So, it shall be."

He chanted low under his breath. As he did, gold tendrils of light lifted from the well spiraling upward and then settling between them. The runes on his skin pulsed. His hands turned hot, searing. She cried out and tried to pull out of his grasp. But he held fast, tightening his grip on her as his voice rose higher and higher with the chant.

The swirling magic settled on their entwined hands. And then, a blinding flash. Heat pounded through her fingers, up her arms. She whimpered, tears blurring her eyes. When he released her, she stumbled backward.

To her horror, her hands glowed bright gold. She gaped at them.

"What—"

"You have the power now."

She blinked, clutching her burning hands to her chest. "How do I—?"

"A hand over the heart will heal the ailment," he said, his voice even and cold. "And now the price will be paid."

Her gaze snapped to his. "Now?"

"When the crown prince is healed, you will return here to me. You will take your place as the Weaver of Wishes."

"What?" The word trickled out her in a roughened whispered. "I don't understand."

"When you take my place, my servitude to the Well of Wishes ends. Forever."

"But—what—does that mean?"

The Well's voice curled through the night like smoke in a tavern. *It means, Serena Windriver, he dies and you take his place.*

Her knees buckled and down she went, landing in the snow and knocking over the lantern. The light snuffed out. She clutched her still glowing hands to her chest as if hiding the magic from the world and herself and knowing she never could.

The stranger stood rooted in place, numb from the cold and what was taken from both of them. His hands curled against the stone rim of the Well until it bit into his palms, burning faintly. He watched, mute, as Serena snatched up her darkened lantern and turned away. Tears slicked her cheeks. Her boots pressed deep into the snow, leaving a fragile trail as she disappeared into the darkness.

Pain lanced through him, sharp enough to make his breath hitch. He should have been glad—his servitude was nearing its end. Death was meant to be a mercy. But this freedom came at the cost of an innocent girl's life. A mortal who would never survive as Weaver of Wishes.

Had it been anyone else, elation might have surged hot and bright through him.

But it wasn't anyone. It was *Serena*.

A beautiful, selfless girl who wanted nothing more than to do the right thing, to heal her father and keep a roof over her head. Her mistake, though, was coming to the Well of Wishes. And yet...he could not name it a mistake. Not when her presence had breathed warmth into his cold, lonely soul.

"The price was too high," he whispered hoarsely.

For that kind of power, the price had to be too high, the Well said.

There was nothing to be done about it, either. Once the crown prince was healed, she was to return here and the exchange of power would happen. His death. Her servitude.

Her teeth had chattered when she asked, *Wh-what about my family?*

They will forget you, he'd said. Cruel. It was too cruel.

Her face had contorted in pain.

And then she whispered, *And if I don't return?*

Your life will still be forfeit. And so will mine.

The words twisted inside him, worse than any blade.

She thought by simply not returning, he would live and she would remain in the village. But the Well always took its due.

You should be happy, dear boy. Your time is ending. No more loneliness. Your dream of release has come true.

"As if that's a consolation," he rasped.

He hated the Well knew his innermost thoughts. Unbidden, Serena's face rose in his mind—not pale and stricken as she had been tonight, but as he longed to see her. Her lips curved in laughter, her eyes bright with mischief, her hair loosened and caught in sunlight. He wanted to see her smile. Gods, he needed it, more than breath.

When he had taken her hands—her small, frigid hands—his own senses had sparked alive again. Her pulse had fluttered against his palms, and for the first time in centuries, something inside him had pulsed, too. Not duty. Not magic. Something far more dangerous. Hope. Desire.

He did not know what it would cost him. What it would cost her.

Ah, but now you have a different dream. A deep, guttural chuckle. *How foolish of you. Did you think this girl, this simple mortal, would want you?*

His jaw locked as he walled off the ache, but the runes throbbed in time with his heart, betraying him. She had come to free him. She had come searching for his true name—a name no one had spoken for centuries. A name lost to time.

He lifted his hand. The runes still glowed faintly, pulsating magic's aftermath he'd forced into her. His throat tightened as he stared at the darkness where she'd vanished.

And then, for the first time since his bondage began, he tilted his head back and whispered his own wish into the wind. Not for release. Not for death.

But for Serena.

CHAPTER 13

The carriage ride to the castle was awkward and uncomfortable.

On the bright side, she did not have to ride with the king and queen. They had already left and were a few hours ahead.

On the not so bright side, she rode with the Grand Duke.

Papa and Maris saw her off at first light. He hugged her, squeezing so hard it was as though he expected her not to return. Maris did her best to look happy for her, but Serena could tell the little wench was pea green with envy.

She didn't sleep at all that night after leaving the stranger behind on the mountain. Since then, her gut had been in a tight knot, her chest ached, and she felt she might be sick at any moment. When King Leonidas told her she was to ride with the Grand Duke, the blood whooshed from her head so fast she saw black dots in her eyes.

"Are you well, my dear? You look pale?" the duke had said. His expression was one of smug satisfaction. Like he was looking forward to exposing her for the fraud she truly was.

She muttered under her breath she was fine as she climbed into the most luxurious carriage she had ever seen.

Her clothes paled in comparison to the richness of the nobles. Her threadbare cloak. Her worn-out shoes. Her woolen dress that had seen better days. All drab in color. At least her wool stockings did not have any holes.

Thankfully, though, her hands had stopped glowing gold. She worried about that at first when she returned home, but by the time she reached their cabin they were back to normal.

Normal.

What was normal anymore? From the moment she made the decision to find the Well of Wishes, her life had been turned upside down.

Across from her, the Grand Duke kept a steely eye on her. Sometimes he gazed out the window. A few times he dozed off. But Serena remained stiff and tall in the plush velvet seat with her hands clasped in her lap. She looked everywhere but at him. But sometimes, she would catch his glittering gaze and it sent a jolt through her.

And not the good kind, either.

Not that kind she felt when she stood in front of the stranger when he looked at her with his mesmerizing eyes. In them, she saw so much depth, so much emotion. He spoke to her silently that way. That last moment they shared together, she was certain he regretted granting her wish.

She regretted it, too.

She glanced down at her clasped hands. Every now and again, a slash of pale sunlight would come through the window of the carriage when it turned a corner. When it did, and the light landed on her hands, she noticed her skin shimmered.

It had never shimmered before.

The carriage rattled over cobblestone streets. Her heart leapt into her throat as her head snapped up and she peered out the window. She was too shy to move toward it, to peer out with unabashed curiosity. If Maris were here, she would do it without hesitation.

"Ah, we are arriving in the capital," the Grand Duke said. The first he'd spoken since they boarded the carriage. He motioned to the window. "Perhaps you'd like to see?"

Serena said nothing as she scooted closer to the edge of the bench to look out. There she got her first glimpse of Ebonvale Palace, rising like a crown upon the distant cliffs. Its spires pierced the wintery sky, pale and ethereal against the swirl of falling snow. Heraldry of plum and gold snapped in the cold wind from every turret, the roaring lion of Leonidas emblazoned proudly as if to remind all who entered whose power reigned here.

They passed through Ebonvale Village. Onlookers lined the streets despite the late hour and the cold to watch the royal processional pass through. Children smiled and waved, their eyes wide and round with wonder.

The carriage headed up the slope of the hill to the gates, through them, and then halted at the front door. Serena waited, shivering. Not from cold. From nerves.

She was unsure of protocol and did not want to misstep. The Grand Duke pulled on his gloves and scooped his fur-lined cloak from the seat next to him. He cast her a glance and then something in his expression shifted from smug to...kindness?

"Here. It appears you need this more than I." He held out his cloak to her.

She gaped at him. "Oh, no, your grace. I couldn't—"

"I insist. Your cloak is not thick enough for the winds on the mountain," he said.

Her jaw clenched. Hesitation clawed through her as she looked from him to the cloak. The fur looked so soft, so warm. It was hard to resist. She reached out and took it from him.

"Thank you, your grace."

The footman opened the carriage door and stood aside. First the Grand Duke exited, then, in another surprising move, he held his hand out to her. With her heart in her throat, she clutched his cloak to her chest and took his hand, stepping out into the late afternoon.

The cold wind immediately bit through her. The duke was correct—the winds were stronger here than in her village. She quickly wrapped the cloak around her, pulling it tight around her shoulders.

"Shall we?" He motioned toward the palace.

She turned to look at it and lost her breath.

The palace was enormous, stretching as far as her eyes could see from one side to the other. Its walls loomed high above her, white stone shimmering with frost, the sheer scale making her feel no bigger than a speck of snow drifting at its feet. The spires pierced the gray sky, vanishing into cloud, and along the ramparts the lion banners of Ebonvale snapped and cracked in the wind, their golden thread flashing like fire against plum silk.

The air was heavy with the mingled scents of wood smoke and horse, and somewhere deeper inside the walls, she thought she caught the faint drift of incense. Guards in gleaming armor lined the gate, their halberds crossed in rigid precision, eyes cold as flint as they watched her. The black iron doors were bound with silver, tall as a forest of trees, and when they groaned open on massive hinges, the sound echoed like thunder in her bones.

Serena clutched the duke's cloak tighter, every instinct telling her to shrink back, but her feet were rooted to the icy cobbles. The palace radiated wealth, command, and judgment, and standing beneath its shadow, she felt as though the walls themselves were deciding whether to let her in...or to crush her where she stood.

"This way, Mistress Serena," the Grand Duke said.

She followed him inside. The moment she crossed the threshold, warmth enveloped her, taking the bite of winter with it.

The hammer-beam ceiling, cut from the finest timber in the realm, in the entry hall soared upward. Brightly lit candelabras were scattered about the room. The marble floor beneath her feet was polished to a high shine. Rich tapestries draped the walls, woven in gold and plum, each depicting the lion of Ebonvale mid-roar. Statues of kings and queens stood in alcoves, their stone eyes watching her as though they expected her to bow. And everywhere—on pillars, on archways, on the steps leading deeper into the palace—there were flourishes of wealth. Gilded carvings, veins of silver set into stone, rugs dyed with colors so deep they looked alive.

Her fingers clenched into the folds of her cloak. She had never imagined such grandeur existed outside of the pages of her father's books. It was beautiful. And terrifying.

Because beauty like this was a reminder—power this great demanded payment. And she had already given too much.

"Mistress Serena, I bid thee welcome to Ebonvale Palace." The booming voice startled her.

She'd been so taken with her surroundings, she never saw the man with the pinched expression approach.

He bowed low in greeting to the Grand Duke. "Your grace."

"What news, Jameson?"

"The physician is with his highness now." Then to her he said, "His majesty requests you attend him at once."

The Grand Duke took her by the elbow. "Then we shall go at once."

She had no idea who Jameson was and didn't think it prudent to ask questions as she was hustled up the grand staircase and through echoing corridors flanked by guards with swords at their sides. She tried her best to keep her gaze forward and not gape at her surroundings—she wasn't here for that, after all.

They halted at a massive chamber door where the man, Jameson, knocked once quickly and then opened the door.

The room smelled of sickness and death. It accosted her. She made a choking sound in the back of her throat and then regretted it when all eyes turned on her. Two guards were on either side of the door and peered at her with bored curiosity. Several attendants were scattered about, on edge and ready to take orders. The king stood to one side, his arms crossed over his thick belly. Next to him, the queen with her pinched expression that said she would rather be anywhere but there.

"Ah, the miracle girl has arrived at last." The king surged forward, holding out a hand to her.

She was suffocating in the duke's thick fur-lined cloak. But propriety and politeness kept her from throwing it off even as sweat trickled down the middle of her back. She had no choice but to take the king's hand. He tugged her toward the bed where a man stood next to it wearing dark robes and a sour face. Dark circles smudged under his eyes. This must be the physician.

In the bed, a young man. Not much older than her. His face was pale and drenched in sweat. His lips were dry and cracked. His skin was yellow. His dark hair was damp and stuck to his head. He wore a white tunic that clung to his thin frame.

He looked like death.

"Who is this?" the man next to the bed said.

"The one I told you about, Ferris," the king said.

Ferris looked down his hawkish nose at her, his dark eyes narrowed and his face lined with suspicion. "Forgive me, your majesty, but you mean to tell me this...girl is going to heal his highness?" He punctuated that with a sniff of haughty derision.

"She is." Then to her, "Aren't you, girl?"

She did not like being called *girl*. But when she realized everyone stared at her waiting for a response, she cleared her throat, dipped a low curtsy to the king. "I will try, your majesty. It is all I can do."

Because, truthfully, she hadn't a clue how the magic in her hands was supposed to work. As she turned toward the bed with the dying crown prince, she hoped the price she paid was worth it. Her palms tingled, and she swore she felt the stranger's voice whisper in the back of her mind.

The price is always too high.

CHAPTER 14

Ferris, the physician, stepped aside to allow her access to the bed. She stared down at the prince's ghastly face, apprehension sweeping through her. Her hands tingled. She curled her fingers into a fist.

She couldn't do this.

Her heart lodged in her throat.

"Well? Get on with it, girl," the king boomed.

She jumped at the king's insistent voice. Her gaze flew to him, his ruddy face, his pinched expression. If she did not do this, he might toss her in the dungeon never to be seen again.

Clutching her hands to her chest, she looked down at the prince once more.

"Sire, forgive me, but perhaps she needs a bit of space to work?" the Grand Duke said.

Serena cut him a glance. His eyes never left hers. Was he...helping her? He tried to motion the group toward the door.

But the king wasn't having it. "If my son dies here and now, I intend to stand here and watch."

Her gut clenched.

She stepped closer to the bed and leaned over him. His breathing was shallow and raspy. His tunic was open a bit at the collar, his chest damp and pasty. She had no reason to think the magic the stranger put in her hands would not work. After all, her other wishes came true. The stranger had said a hand over the heart would heal him, but she thought that might be too easy for the onlookers to accept.

Instead, she made a show of it.

"I will...need to examine him." Her voice was small and quiet in the room.

With a shaking hand, she reached out to him and placed her palm on his forehead. Gods, his skin was cold and clammy. The moment she touched him, his eyes flew open.

Blue eyes, the color of the ocean, peered back at her. Confusion edged away the surprise.

"Who..." he started, but his voice gave out.

"I'm here to help," she whispered.

"I don't know you."

She granted him a smile. "No. My name is Serena."

The prince closed his eyes again and expelled a breath. "Serena...Pretty name."

Her heart fluttered. "May I try to help you, your highness?"

His dark head nodded against the pillow as his eyes remained closed.

In the lamplight of the room, her skin continued to shimmer. But it was no longer muted. Now, it had started to faintly glow.

A hand over the heart. That's what the stranger had said. And so, taking a deep breath, she flattened her right palm on his chest. Beneath her hand, his heart beat in an unnatural rhythm. Fast—slow—fast—slow. As she held her hand there, though, nothing happened. Her hand did not glow like it did when the stranger gave her the power.

Perhaps she needed both hands. She placed her left on top of her right. Still nothing happened. She bit the edge of her lip.

Movement in the room. The shuffle of feet. She sensed the Grand Duke edging closer to peer at her hands on the prince's chest. She stole a glance and saw his face was pinched with a smug expression. One that said he was glad she was proving to him she was what he thought—a fraud.

She was not a fraud.

Well, she was. Truly. But—

You have the power now.

But perhaps there was more to it than simply *having* the power. Perhaps she had to make a wish. Like she had to the stranger. She closed her eyes to shut out the smug face of the Grand Duke and the deathly pale face of the prince. She thought only of healing, of banishing whatever ailment vexed him.

"I have the power," she murmured. "I have the power to heal him. To take away his sickness. I wish for the prince to be well."

Her hands burned. Her bones felt as though they were on fire, her blood molten gold. The power wasn't hers—it was his, the stranger's—and she feared she would shatter beneath it.

Sucking a sharp breath, she peeked through her eyelids. Her hands were engulfed in gold, glowing so bright they lit up the entire room. She squeezed her eyes closed again. Behind her, a scuffle. Shouting. Voices. The queen's. The king's. Angry. Frightened. The *shing* of a sword as it was ripped from a scabbard.

They thought she was killing him.

"Be at ease," she said, her voice calmer than she felt. Though who she spoke to—herself, the prince, or the others—she did not know.

Inside, her nerves jangled, her gut clenched into a tight knot. Her heart raced. Her pulse pounded a roar in her ears.

When she opened her eyes again, the prince's body was encased in the golden glow from head to toe. Beneath her palm, his heart slowed to a normal pace. One beat. Two. For one terrible heartbeat she thought she'd stolen his last breath. And then his chest rose, his eyes flung open, and the world righted itself. He sat up so violently, it knocked her hands away. She stumbled back a step from the bed, curling her hands to her chest, clutching them into fists.

Immediately, color returned to the prince's face. His breath see-sawed in and out of him. His wild eyes peered about the room.

Silence descended for a long moment.

And then it was broken with the queen crying out. She ran to the other side of the bed and flung herself at her son, wrapping her arms around his shoulders and pulling him into a tight embrace, her face streaked with tears.

Serena turned away, feeling as though it was an intimate moment she should not witness. When she did, she saw the pinched expression of the Grand Duke as he glared at her. Next to her, Ferris gaped. Then he snapped out of it to shove her aside and pick up his medical kit.

"I must examine him, my queen," Ferris said.

He was already plugging the listening horn of polished silver into his ear to check the man's heart. The queen released the crown prince and stepped aside as Ferris pressed it to his chest. He moved it up, down, side to side. Then he pressed two fingers against his wrist, checking his pulse.

"Well, Ferris? Is he healed? Will he live?" the king asked.

"His pulse is steady. His heart is strong." He pulled the horn from his ear and dropped it into his medical kit. Steely eyes pinned her for the briefest of moments, then he turned to the king. "I believe he will live."

A collective sigh escaped into the room. But Serena still felt the eyes of the Grand Duke on her shining with skepticism. Was he still plotting to expose her as a fraud behind those steely eyes?

The king dashed around the bed. Before she realized what was happening, he enveloped her in a bear hug and a jolly laugh in her ear that vibrated through his big body.

She let him, but inside she was hollow. This miracle was no gift. It was a debt, and the Well always came to collect.

When he pulled her away, he held her at arm's length. "You truly are the miracle girl!"

"Well, sire, I—"

"Lachland," he interrupted, turning to the Grand Duke, "make sure this darling thing has a room. The finest. And, by the gods, give her something decent to wear. And perhaps a bath."

The Grand Duke bowed low. "As you say, your majesty." Then he scurried out of the room to do his bidding.

The king turned back to her, his cheeks ruddy and his eyes twinkling with joy. "You'll stay with us a few days, of course."

It didn't sound like she had a choice. She nodded, thinking of Papa and Maris and...the stranger.

And the bargain that bound her life to the Well of Wishes.

The king grinned, then snapped his fingers in quick succession. A moment later, a servant was curtsying low at his side.

"Clean her up, will you?" He handed her off as though she were nothing more than a soiled towel.

The woman gave a nod and motioned for her to follow.

Serena cast one more glance backward to the crown prince as his mother fawned over him and the others chattered away about what they'd witnessed.

Apprehension and dread clutched her.

"Come with me, milady," the servant said in a soft tone.

With her heart in her throat, she had no choice but to follow. Straight into the lion's den.

CHAPTER 15

Serena was given the finest room in the royal apartments as well as a full wardrobe at her disposal, a bath whenever she wanted it, and food. Her belly had never been so full nor had she ever slept on something so fine. Her room overlooked the gardens that were bursting with blooms—even in winter—and an immaculately kept hedge maze. Undisturbed snow blanketed the ground giving it a wondrous, enchanted feel.

The days passed, and the crown prince—who was named Edgar—recovered from his terrible illness. A malady no one, not even the royal physician, was able to explain.

But as time went on, her apprehension and restlessness grew. She would return to the village and when she did, payment to the Well was due.

Her life for his.

Still, she wondered about his true name. What was it? Where to find it? She'd made a haphazard search in Papa's meager library but had found nothing about the tithe the stranger paid—eternal servitude. What had he done to deserve such a fate?

One morning, after the maid helped her dress and tie back her hair, there was a knock on her door. The maid scurried to answer it. When she pulled it open, she immediately curtsied low.

Standing on the other side of the door was Prince Edgar.

He looked hale and healthy. His color had returned. His dark hair was perfectly combed—longer and shaggy about his face, touching the high collar of his midnight blue jacket trimmed in silver with silver buttons. He wore dark pants and shiny boots. Now that he was well, she saw life in those ocean-blue eyes and it made her smile.

She had done that.

No. She hadn't.

The stranger had given her the power to do that.

The servant girl rose and stepped aside, keeping her eyes downcast. But Serena looked at him with unabashed adoration. He was handsome, to be sure, with high cheekbones, a pointed chin, broad shoulders and chest.

Maris would love him.

"May I enter?" His warm voice wrapped around her like a hug.

"Yes, of course, your highness." She dipped a curtsy.

To the servant girl, he said, "You may leave us."

When she was out of the room, he stepped inside and gazed at her with an appreciation she did not deserve. Today, she was dressed in a fine gown of pale violet. The long sleeves came to a point on the backs of her hands. Her slippers were new—not at all like her well-worn boots that had stomped through the snow and mud.

"I came to offer my thanks," he said.

"No thanks are necessary, your highness."

"Please. Won't you call me Edgar?" He moved closer to her. So close, in fact, his scent wafted to her. Something clean and bright and utterly alluring.

"I don't think I should, your highness."

He grinned, though she was aware of the frustration wafting from him. "As you wish, then. My attendants tell me it was quite the spectacle."

She tipped her head to the side. "Healing you?"

"Yes." A smile pulled at the corners of his lips. He leaned in and dropped his voice to a fake whisper. "They think you're a witch."

She laughed, albeit a nervous one. "I assure you, I am no witch."

"That's what I told them."

He reached for her hand, then, taking it in his warm one. Such a contrast from when she had healed him and his skin was cold and clammy. His thumb swept over the back of her hand, sending a tingling sensation through her. Her pulse jumped at the warmth of his touch, but guilt pricked her skin. Another's touch lingered in memory—stronger, sadder, bound to her in a way this prince could never be.

"I'm grateful to you, Serena Windriver. Words cannot express my thanks."

She did not know why it shocked her that he knew her full name. "You're welcome, your highness. I was glad to do it."

Even as she said it, the lie burned through her.

His thumb continued to stroke her hand, his gaze never leaving hers. "They tell me you are the miracle girl."

"I am not," she said. "I'm just a girl."

In fact, once she had healed the prince, the shimmering of her skin had disappeared. It was as though she poured every ounce of magic the stranger gave her into the crown prince to cure him. And that was fine by her. She didn't want the magic lingering in her hands.

"Well, just a girl. Would you take a stroll with me? I'm restless after convalescing for so long and I'd enjoy some company."

He was so different from his father. He seemed more congenial and sweet instead of abrasive and harsh and demanding. Perhaps that was what was required of a king. Edgar had not been subjected to ruling a kingdom yet.

The prince glanced toward the window where gray light slashed inside. "It's a dreadful morning though. Too cold to walk in the gardens but I could show you the palace."

How could she refuse? "If you like."

A smile tugged at the corners of his lips. He tucked her hand into the crook of his elbow. "Where shall we go first? The armory? The ballroom? The library?"

That caught her attention. Her breath caught in her throat. She thought of her father's books of folklore and poetry and how she'd read about the man who made three wishes. As her gut clenched and a tingling sensation swept through her, the idea caught. Perhaps, in the king's library, she'd find something about the stranger. Some way to break his curse and free him. Even if it meant she could not free herself.

"You have a library?"

"Oh, yes. A grand one at that." He beamed, proud. "It's one of my favorite rooms."

"May we start there?"

He placed his hand on top of hers. "As you wish, my lady."

As they left the room, flanked by two guards, her heart clawed to her throat. The prince was charming and chattered on as they headed down the corridor to the grand staircase. But she was too distracted by her own thoughts as hope bloomed in her chest.

"Wouldn't you agree, my lady?" he asked.

She blinked, pulling herself back to her thoughts and cast him a sideways glance. He was looking at her with a curiosity. She hadn't a clue what she was supposed to agree.

"I'm sorry, your highness. I was lost in my own thoughts." She flushed, her cheeks hot as she turned her gaze forward once again.

He chuckled, a deep sound in his chest. "I said, despite the cold, I prefer winter. Do you agree?"

"Oh." The word came out in a breath. "It's dreadfully cold. I find Spring to be lovely with all the new blooms and the land renewing itself."

"Spring is nice, but I confess I much prefer winter to any other season."

"Why is that, your highness?"

"Because I can remain inside with my books. I'm not much for tourneys."

"My father loves to read, too," she said. Because she couldn't think of anything else to say.

"Does he?" He sounded happy about that. "What does he like to read?"

"Old tales mostly. Folklore and myths. He has a small collection. A few books," she said.

"Well, then, we shall have to remedy that. Ah! Here we are!"

She didn't know what that meant—did the crown prince intend to give her father books?—but was unable to ask as they arrived at a set of large double doors. The prince released her and pushed them open, the iron hinges groaning with the effort.

His eyes were alight with excitement as he led her inside, proud to show off the room.

Serena stepped through the door and halted, gazing around the room that had shelves of books soaring high to the ceiling. It was a cozy room, too. A hearth on one end with plush furniture that invited the reader to sit, read, and stay awhile. The floor was covered in a thick jewel-toned rug stretching from corner to corner, wall to wall. Walls that did not host bookshelves were adorned with oil paintings of the royal family.

It was everything she'd ever dreamed of for her father, and for a fleeting heartbeat, she wished she could be the girl who belonged here. But she wasn't. The Well had seen to that.

"Do you love it?" the crown prince asked.

"It is amazing," she breathed.

He took her by the hand, holding it in his warm one. "I'm glad. Shall we choose a book?"

Her gaze flicked from the shelves back to him. He looked so happy, so jovial, so excited to sit here and read alone...with her. How could she say no?

"If that's what you'd like, your highness."

His hand tightened on hers as he drew closer. "I find quiet solitude with a book and easy companionship with a lady is what I'd like. What do you like to read?"

Truthfully, she wasn't much of a reader. That was Papa. He was the one with his nose always stuck between the pages. Her life was far too busy to enjoy such a leisurely activity. There was the baking and the cooking, the gardening and the sewing. All to make sure they stayed warm and fed and clothed. The prince, though, lived a life of luxury and would never understand her hardships.

Or the price she paid to be here with him.

But, with a massive library at her disposal, she had one chance to change all that.

"Do you have any books about the Fae?"

His brows winged upward. "You have an inquisitive mind, I see. I like that about you. We have a few. I'll show you."

While she picked several books about Fae folklore, he rang for tea and had a servant built a warm fire. Once he had a book about sea-faring adventures in hand, they settled down together in the seating area to read. It could not have felt more domestic. And, for once, Serena craved it.

But as she cracked open the first book, she knew it was not to be. And for the first time, Serena wondered if saving him meant damning herself.

CHAPTER 16

Hours later, Serena's eyes were dry and gritty but she was determined not to give up. Prince Edgar, however, had long since dozed off, his book open on his chest. The gentle rise and fall of his chest indicated he was in deep in sleep.

It gave her ample time to continue her research. Determination was the only thing driving her now. She *had* to find the name of the stranger.

With a glance over her shoulder, she saw the prince continued to doze. Likely he was still recovering from his illness and he needed the rest. She set aside the volume she was reading and returned to the bookshelf where she'd found that one.

Then she saw it.

The Hidden Courts: Folklore and Forgotten Histories of the Fae

How had she not seen it before? With a shaking hand, she pulled the thick book off the shelf. It was bound in a deep green leather, its cover tooled with golden knotwork that seemed to shimmer and glow under the lamplight. With her heart beating rapidly, she headed back to the chair by the fire and opened it. Excitement seared through her.

She flipped pages, looking for...what, she did not know. Something. Anything that would give her what she needed. Then she stopped on the chapter called *The Weaver of Wishes*. A quiet gasp escaped her. She'd found it.

> *There are tales of the Weaver of Wishes, a Fae prince of the Seelie Court, once known by the name Caedon Lyserian. Proud and noble, he broke the first law of Fae magic—gifting power without barter, giving freely to one he loved. For this, the Well of Wishes bound him in eternal servitude, to weave what others desired at the cost of memory, secret, or soul. Legends say his curse may be undone only if a mortal speaks his true name, for a name is both lock and key in the realm of the Fae.*

She sucked in a breath and then his name escaped her on a whisper. "Caedon."

The name curled over her tongue like a dangerous secret. For a moment, the air in the library seemed to thicken, and she swore the flames in the hearth flickered higher. Unexpected tears burned her eyes. She'd found it. She's found *him*. He was not merely a Fae. He was a Fae Prince of the Seelie Court.

Shaking with her newfound discovery, she closed the book with a thump and clutched it against her chest.

The noise startled the prince awake. He sat up, the book sliding from his chest to his lap as he blinked sleepy ocean-blue eyes. For a moment, he looked disoriented as he glanced around the room and then looked at her. A sleepy grin tugged his lips.

"You're still here," he said. "You're shivering. Are you cold?"

He rose to stoke the fire.

She wasn't shivering because she was cold. She was shivering because she had *found the answer*. She couldn't tell him that.

"A bit," she lied, teeth chattering.

Once the fire was going again, he rose and turned to her, his brows creased. "How long was I asleep?"

"A while," she said. "I think you needed the rest."

He noticed the pile of books next to her and grinned. "It must have been a good long while if you've read all those."

His stomach rumbled then, and he flushed. "My apologies, my lady. You must be famished. Could I escort you to dinner after we change?"

Court rules. They always dressed for dinner.

Serena got to her feet. Admittedly, she was hungry, too, but she would never say so to the prince directly. It was the least of her worries. She was much more interested in finding out the stranger's name. And now she had it. She continued to clutch the book to her chest.

"I wonder, your highness, if I could borrow this book?"

"Of course," he said without hesitation or asking what it was. He held out his arm to her. "Shall we?"

She took it. He was so formal, it was difficult for her to relax in his presence. As he escorted her back to her room, her mind whirled.

Caedon. *His name was Caedon.*

Caedon Lyserian. A Fae Prince of the Seelie Court. Weaver of Wishes. Ruler of her heart.

The thought jolted her. She hadn't expected it. Nor had she expected to have any sort of feeling for this man who had come to her aid on more than one occasion. She had no right to feel anything for him and yet...

Yet, her heart fluttered as she turned his name over and over again in her mind.

She couldn't believe she was able to find it in the massive library in the palace. It was as though it was here, waiting for her to discover. Waiting for her to learn his name and bring him back to life. Release him from his terrible bondage.

Now more than ever, she wanted to flee the palace and return to her village, climb the mountain, and announce to the Well of Wishes she knew his name. If it saved him from certain death, she would do it. Because he had saved her.

At her door, the prince bid her farewell with the promise to return. She nodded, anxious to get past dinner and back to her room so she could practice saying Caedon's name aloud.

The hours crawled. Dinner dragged on. She did her best to pay attention, smile and nod, and reply when asked questions. But dining with the royal family was never something she aspired to do. Maris, on the other hand, would have loved it.

The prince was attentive. Sitting next to her. Keeping her close. Leaning in to whisper when his father said something brash.

A sudden awareness struck her. The way he sat so close. The way his hand brushed hers when there was no need. The way he cast her surreptitious glances and gave her soft smiles.

Oh, gods.

He liked her.

Perhaps it was merely because she'd healed him and his affections were displaced. She hoped that was the case.

Her sister's face came crashing back to her. How she had that dreamy look of hope when she learned the king was coming to the village. How she hoped he was coming to pick a bride. And what did Serena do? She scoffed at the thought and dismissed it.

And yet...here he was. The crown prince sitting next to her with his smiles, casting her adoring looks.

She needed to put a stop to this. She pressed a hand against her forehead.

"My lady, are you well?" the prince asked, concern edging his tone.

This was her chance. She gave him a weak smile. "I'm afraid I have a bit of a headache. I think I'd like to retire."

She pushed back from the table. The prince did the same.

"I'll escort you."

Would this never end? She forced a smile and took his outstretched hand, aware of all the eyes on her as they departed the palatial dining room.

When they were out of earshot of the room, he said, "Thank you for spending time with me today."

She gave him a questioning glance. "In the library?"

He nodded. "No one has ever spent that much time with me before."

Something about that made her heart squeeze. Then a wave of guilt washed over her. She merely wanted to go to the library so she could find the answers she needed about Caedon.

"I was glad to do it," she said with a smile.

"You truly are special, my lady," he said.

She cringed but kept her face impassive so as not to give away her inner thoughts. "I don't think so, your highness."

"I do. You're brave to come here. You saved me."

Gods, why did he have to say such things? Did he not understand she had no choice? That she could not refuse the call from the king himself? That she felt she put her life and her family in jeopardy if she refused?

She said nothing. She kept her eyes forward as they continued to walk. Relief pressed through her to see the two guards standing outside her chamber door. And though she saved the prince and was given the privilege—no, the honor—of being in the royal apartments, it was clear they did not truly trust her.

At the door, she halted and turned to the prince. "Thank you for escorting me back."

It occurred to her then that the prince was escorting her to keep an eye on her, to make sure she went where she was supposed to go at all times.

"It was my pleasure, my lady." He took her hand in his, held it for a long moment, his eyes searching hers. He looked as though he wanted to say something more.

Her heart kicked up speed, pounding against her ribcage. "If there's nothing more, your highness?"

He squeezed her hand, started to release her, then held fast once again. He pressed a kiss against the inside of her wrist. Right above her racing pulse. She wanted to recoil, to snatch her hand away, but she didn't. When his gaze met hers again, she saw delight in them.

He'd misconstrued her racing pulse as affection when, in fact, it was fear. Fear that she would not be able to escape this prison of her own making.

"Tomorrow, will you ride out with me?"

"Ride, your highness?"

"I know it's cold out, but I would like to spend some time with you. Alone. I have…" He paused, pressing his lips together as though he was unable to find the right words. "I have something I'd like to ask you."

No. *No.* She didn't want him to ask her anything. But she did not refuse him. "A ride sounds lovely."

"Good. I'll make sure they bring you warm clothes." He released her hand.

"Thank you, your highness." She dipped a curtsy.

Then she entered her room and closed the door with a snap, leaning against the solid wood until she heard his receding footsteps.

What in the stars above could he want to ask her?

She pushed away the thought. She knew, if she was being honest with herself. And she could not accept it. She *could not.* She had a promise to keep.

Her gaze landed on the green book she'd left in the center of her bed. She rushed to it, then, picked it up and flipped to the page where she read again the story of Caedon. She ran her fingers over the printed ink and then tried out his name on her tongue.

"Caedon Lyserian."

She liked the way it sounded, the way it felt when she said it. The way her heart raced when she did.

"I have found you," she whispered. She read on, "*He broke the first law of Fae magic.* What was that, Caedon? What did you do?"

Serena kicked off her slippers and climbed into the bed, holding the book. She read more, in the hopes she would learn the truth. But there was nothing in the book that gave her that answer. After a time, she fell asleep, clutching the book and dreaming of the Fae prince who was bound into servitude for all eternity. She dreamed of the Well of Wishes, golden magic tendrils curling upward into the night, lighting it up.

Your time is ended, Serena Windriver. The wish has been granted. The bargain must be paid.

"But...my family...I haven't—"

That does not concern me. You have tasted power. You have taken what is not yours. Now, return. The Well will claim you. Your breath, your blood, your name.

She whimpered, trying to pull herself out of sleep. But something held her there. As though the Well itself had invaded her dream.

You cannot hide. You cannot flee. The Weaver waits, the hour draws near. Come to the mountain, Serena Windriver. It is time.

She jolted awake, heart pounding, sitting upright so quickly the book slid off her chest and off the bed, thumping on the floor. The room was still and quiet. Only the dying embers in the hearth glowed there.

And she knew then what she had to do.

Return to the mountain, speak his name, and risk everything before the Well claimed her first.

CHAPTER 17

Dawn broke across the sky, bleeding through the wintery clouds in a brilliant display of fiery orange and yellow.

Even as she noticed the vivid display, she pushed her horse to go faster. She needed to put as much distance between her and the palace as possible.

After the dream of the Well, she had quickly dressed in her old clothes, slipping on her shoes and pulling on a thick fur-lined cloak. She had tucked the book under her arm and then turned toward the door, her heart in the throat.

She had lied to the castle guards, telling them the prince asked her to meet him in the stables.

She had stolen a horse—she knew how to saddle one herself—and she had ridden away into the dead of night with nothing but the book in the saddlebags. No food. No water. No other clothes.

As she rode, that phantom voice she'd heard in her dream still haunted her.

Come to me, Serena Windriver.

Now, she was nearly to the village. It would be waking at this early hour. Even in the dead of winter. As she approached, she saw gray smoke curling from chimneys and faint yellow light glowing in windows. But she did not stop.

As much as she wanted to stop and hug Papa and Maris, she did not. She continued, skirting the outer edge of the village to, hopefully, go unnoticed.

At the foot of the mountain, she dismounted. The horse's neck had a fine sheen of sweat along it. She had ridden it far too hard, but she had to get out the palace and return to the village. She knew, by now, her absence would be discovered. By now, the king's guards would be dispatched to find her and bring her back. She would be branded a witch and a fraud for why else would she run from the prince?

"Godspeed, old girl," she muttered to the horse.

She pulled the book from the saddlebag, gave the horse one last pat, and then turned toward the mountain. She climbed, her breath crystalizing in front of her. She pushed herself to hurry, making her legs burn and her heart race. Her only thought was getting to the top, was finding *him*. The stranger.

No.

Caedon. That was his name.

He waited for her when she arrived at the top. The hood of his cloak was down to reveal his face in the early morning light. His eyes, so bright, pierced her the second she halted, trying to catch her breath, clutching the book to her chest.

His expression was one of sorrow, of regret, of pain.

Ah, so the girl has returned, the voice of the Well said. It sounded delighted by her arrival.

"Yes, I returned. As I promised." But her gaze never left Caedon's.

"It is time, then," he said.

"No, wait, please. I have one last request."

He lifted a brow, curious.

The Well said, agitated, *The bargain was struck. The payment is due, girl.*

She ignored it. "There is something I must know. Grant me this one last..." She paused, pressed her lips together. Then continued, "...favor."

The girl wishes for a favor?

Caedon swallowed hard, his throat working.

There is no time—

"I will give you my life," she snapped and glared at the Well. "You can give me one last moment with the Weaver."

Silence and then a low, malicious chuckle. *Very well, girl.*

Her gaze swung back to his. He regarded coolly, looking impressed she dared snap back at the Well.

"I have nothing to offer you," he said.

She took a deep breath and blew it out. It misted in the air around her as she continued to clutch the book to her chest, hope rising there. "You said once the price is always too high. But you never told me why you're here. What you did. Who cursed you."

Faint morning light flickered in this blue-green depths as he glanced away, unable to look at her. He said nothing for a long time. His jaw worked, as though he held back the words that wanted to erupt.

At last, he spoke, his voice low and rough and guarded. "I loved a girl once. Mortal. Not unlike you."

Serena's heart lurched.

"She lived in a small village on the edge of the forest," he continued, his gaze drifting into memory. "She was kind. Smart. Full of joy. Her laugh was bright. Her smile was infectious. She smelled like wind and sun and everything lovely. Her hair was the color of a copper. But her people were dying. A fever swept through, claiming lives and threatening those she loved. She came to the Well." He paused here, swallowing hard. "She begged for help, but had nothing to give."

She understood then. Because, once, she was that girl. "You gave it to her freely."

He gave a sharp nod. "I broke the law. Fae magic is never free. Wishes are bargains and there is always a price, Serena. But I loved her. And I could not stand to see her and her family suffer. I gave her what she asked. Freely. Without a price. Her family was saved. I was condemned."

Her throat tightened. The edge of the book bit into her fingers.

"The Seelie Court called it treason. To give freely was to upset the balance, to unravel all bargains. And so, they bound me to the Well to become the Weaver of Wishes. To claim the price and deposit it there." He jabbed a finger to the Well.

Serena's mouth went dry. "What happened to her?"

"The magic had been too strong. It destroyed her. And I remained."

"I-I—"

When she started to speak, he moved toward her, taking her by the upper arms, and pulling her close. "I swore I would never love again. But then you came with too much courage and too much kindness. You foolish, beautiful girl. You look at me—like that—and I remember." His voice cracked. He paused, swallowed. "I remember what it's like to feel alive."

Silence fell between them. He dropped his hands and stepped back, turning away from her, toward the Well. His gloved hands leaned on the edge of the stone as he stared down into the darkness. She moved next to him and reached for him, her hand shaking. She placed it on his arm to gain his attention.

When he looked at her with those blue-green eyes, she saw the torture, the regret, the sorrow.

"Then let me be the one who frees you. Not by forgetting. But by remembering your name."

His eyes went wide as he stiffened, his back straight. "Serena—"

"I know who you are. You are Caedon Lyserian, Fae Prince of the Seelie Court."

As she said it, frost cracked along the Well's rim. It rumbled as a wicked scream ripped from its depths. The ground shook their feet.

No! It shouted. *NO! NO! NO! He's mine!*

Caedon sucked in a deep breath, the cold air burning his lungs as he glanced at the Well, the glittering gold magic swirling up from the depths. It had been delighted to take his life, but she had foiled that.

"Not anymore," she said with such vehemence it shocked him. His eyes swung back to her. Defiance lit her face. "Shall I say it again? Caedon Lyserian."

His name rolled off her tongue. And it was such a sweet sound. Something he had not heard in more than an age. His heart swelled then thudded against his chest, echoing in the hollow chambers of his soul. *His name.* For so long he had been only Weaver, only shadow, only servitude. Now he was himself.

Awe cracked him open, sharp and sweet. In his bones, he felt the chains snap. Each link exploding outward, centuries of magic unwinding from his veins in molten rivers. He staggered, breath tearing free as if he'd been drowning all this time and only now found air.

She had done it. And for one glorious moment, he was free.

He stripped off the gloves, flinging them to the ground, and watched as the golden runes etched in his skin faded to nothing, disappearing as though it had never happened. He held them up, gaping at them in wonder.

His eyes met her bright blue ones shimmering with tears. Her face creased with elation. She took a step toward him, reaching for him.

Then she gasped, her body seizing and bowing backward. A cry ripped from her as the golden light shot from the Well. Gold tendrils wrapped her like the chains that had once bound him. Then, the same runes that branded him were etched into her delicate skin, glowing and burning brightly as it had the day he paid his due.

And now she had paid.

Terror licked at the edges of his joy. The Well would not release so easily. The horror nearly broke him. To free him was to doom her.

The Well laughed, a deep dark laugh full of malice and hate and revenge.

She will take your sentence, Weaver. She will pay YOUR price since she robbed me of the one pleasure I had in a millennium—the thought of your death.

"No! Serena!"

The book she held tumbled from her arms, landing with a muffled thud at her feet. She pitched forward, falling in the snow. He wasn't fast enough to catch her. She writhed in agony, the light searing through her veins and lighting her up from the inside. He knew that pain. He could not let her bear it.

He scooped her into his arms. Her teeth chattered as she looked at him, the brightness fading from her eyes. She lifted a hand as if to touch his cheek, then saw the burning, glowing fire in her hands and her face crumpled.

"I-I saved you. You're free. Caedon."

Oh, *gods*, but he would give anything to reverse what was done to her. What was taken from him.

"Yes, I'm free."

She dies, you fool. I will have my due, the Well insisted.

He ignored it. It had taunted him for centuries and he was done with it. Caedon brushed his hand over her cold cheek.

"No more bargains, Serena Windriver," he murmured. "Only this."

And then he kissed her. Not as the cursed Weaver, but as the prince he had once been. And for the first time in centuries, the Well fell silent.

CHAPTER 18

The moment his lips met hers, it wasn't magic he felt but something older, purer. Heat blooming through his frozen veins, thawing centuries of loneliness in a single heartbeat. Light burst from the Well, not gold but searing blue-white, scouring the shadows from the tree line. For the first time in an age, Caedon felt the world hold its breath.

In his arms Serena trembled, the golden runes flickering and dimming on her skin. The Well growled, a sound like stones grinding in a deep chasm, spitting threads of gold as it tried to recover what it had stolen. But its grip slid off her like water.

Caedon realized then the kiss was not only love. It was a choice. *His* choice. His first true act of freely given magic.

The Well emitted a long, low growl. It rumbled, growing restless, trying to belch out the golden magic to get what it wanted. *Her.*

You tried to take her from me, prince, but she is still mine. And I will have her, the Well raged. *I will take her true name and make her forget you.*

"You won't," he snapped. "You can't. Because I've already said it—Serena Windriver."

The world shivered around him.

The price must be paid!

"Bargains built on cruelty and theft are not binding," he snapped.

He understood. More deeply than he ever had. Love was the only magic stronger than the Well's hunger. And though the golden magic swirled upward from the deep, dark chasm of the well, it could not latch onto her.

Or him.

The Well railed against this.

Because he felt love and admiration for her—this small girl he held cradled in his arms.

"You cannot break this bond we have," he said.

It sneered. *And what is that, PRINCE?*

"She sacrificed herself to release me, as I gave myself to her freely. That is the only bond stronger than you and your hunger."

The frost that had coated the rim of the well thickened. The golden tendrils trying to escape dissipated, snuffing out. And beneath him, the mountain shifted. A loud crack. The stone well split down the center, creating a deep fracture. It groaned one last time and then...there was silence.

Only the sound of the wind fluttering the treetops remained. And somewhere, in the distance, the twitter of a bird.

He had not heard birdsong in a century.

Serena stirred as she drew in a breath and then her eyes fluttered open. She looked at him in confusion. A breath escaped between her lips as she blinked, understanding and awareness lighting there. A smile tipped the corners of her mouth.

"Caedon."

The laugh bubbled up from his lungs and escaped before he could stop it. He cradled her against him in a hug, inhaling her deep scent—of snow and horse and leather. When he pulled back, he kissed her again.

This time, she kissed him back.

A deep, sweet kiss that stole his breath and made his heart tumble in his chest. A kiss of forever. A kiss that meant he would never let her go. She was his.

When they broke, she pressed a hand against his smooth cheek.

They both noticed, then, the golden light of the runes had faded from her skin, leaving behind faint scars. Proof she had paid the price. She sat up, leaving the cocoon of his arms as she examined her skin. Her gaze snapped to his.

"It happened, then, truly. I was—" she started, then pressed her lips together, as though unsure what she wanted to say.

"The Well tried but did not succeed."

"How?" Her brows drew together in question.

He caught her hand in his and delighted in the way her fine-boned fingers fit into his palm. "You saved me, Serena. Once by speaking my name." He lifted her fingers to his lips, pressed a kiss there. "And once by reminding me how to love."

He said this so simply, it sent heat coiling through her belly. He was not jesting. He meant it. Her mouth turned dry as she swallowed but she found she could not look away from his blue-green eyes.

"Oh." A breath shuddered out of her.

She didn't know what else to say. So instead, she tugged her hand from his and pressed it against his smooth cheek. From the moment she decided to find his true name, she never imagined she would end up in his arms on the top of the mountain wanting to kiss him again.

"I give it to you freely, Serena, if you will have it."

The words were sweet, endearing, and made her heart thump. "Can a Fae prince truly love a mortal girl like me?"

"He can. And he does."

"Then this mortal girl will take not only his love, but him as well. As he is."

He smiled. It was the first time she'd ever seen him smile. And for the first time, she noticed he wore no gloves. When she looked at his hands, they were devoid of the golden runes. Like hers, they had the marks that he, too, had once paid the price.

She glanced at the well, then. "Is it...?" Her words drifted away.

"No more."

"Good," she said and meant it. "No more wishes. No more bargains."

He helped her to her feet. They stood together, for a long moment, looking at the well. Then she saw the book half buried in the snow and bent to pick it up. She held it out to him, the gold embossed letters still glittering in the faint morning light.

"I found the answer in this," she said.

He peered down at it. "*The Hidden Courts: Folklore and Forgotten Histories of the Fae.*" His gaze lifted back to hers. "Where did you get it?"

"In the king's library." As she said it, the blood drained from her head. "I took it. And..." She sucked in a breath, blew it out. Her nerves jangled. "I left in the middle of the night. I'm sure the king's men will be looking for me."

"Because you took a book?" He sounded confused.

"Because I healed the crown prince and...I think he was going to ask for my hand."

It sounded absurd even to her own ears. But she could not stop thinking of what the prince said to her. *I have something I'd like to ask you.*

"Oh," he said.

Her head snapped up to him. "I would have said no."

He grinned. "I'm glad. But, Serena, they will want to know why you ran in the middle of the night." There was a hint of worry in his words.

"Yes. That's why I must see to my father and sister." Her gaze drifted toward the village nestled against the base of the mountain. "The king's men will look for me there first."

Caedon moved closer to her, his warmth radiating from him. "I worry for you."

She looked up at him, a smile pulling at her mouth. "I will be fine. I have to face it. At least now I know I am not alone."

"You'll never be alone as long as I have breath."

Without thinking, she stepped to him and placed her head on his chest. The steady beat of his heart was beneath her ear. He wrapped his arms around her, holding her tight.

"Whatever happens?" she asked.

"Whatever happens."

Warmth swept through her and coiled low in her belly. She wanted to stay there forever, but she knew, she could not. She moved away from him and turned toward the village. Toward home.

"I will find you again," he said, and it sounded like a vow.

"You better." And that was her vow.

As weariness pounded through her, she began the long descent home.

Caedon watched her vanish into the white silence, each step stealing a piece of him with her.

A piece of his heart.

When at last the mountain hid her from sight, he turned to the wind, letting it hear his vow to the only soul who would ever truly matter.

"No more bargains. No more cages. Only freedom. I am yours, Serena Windriver. Always."

And the vow carried, echoing through snow and sky, binding him not to a curse, but to her.

Want More Magic?
Visit the Five Towers!

Amidst the shadows of thievery, a single crystal holds the power to unlock her destiny. But will the ultimate power be her ultimate undoing?

The Sorcerer's Daughter

Get it in ebook, audio, and paperback here!

ALSO BY MICHELLE MILES

Age of Wizards (Epic Fantasy)

In the Tower of the Wizard King

On the Hunt for the Wizard King

Dragon Protectors (Paranormal Shifter Romance)

Desiring the Dragon Lord

Seducing the Dragon Knight

Tempting Her Dragon Bodyguard

Dragon Protectors Book Collection (Books 1-3)

Dream Walker (Urban Fantasy)

Call of the Dark

Blood and Bone

Flame and Fury

Smoke and Ashes

Light of the World

Dream Walker Collection (Books 1-5)

Divine Heir: Dream Walker Origins

Enchanted Realms (YA Fantasy Romance)

Once Upon a Midnight Clear (Cinderella)

Once Upon True Love's Kiss (Snow White)

Once Upon an Enchanted Kiss (Sleeping Beauty)

Once Upon an Enchanted Castle (Beauty and the Beast)

Once Upon a Midnight Dreary (Poe's The Raven)

Enchanted Realms Related Novellas

Once Upon an Ancient Curse (Red Riding Hood)

Once Upon a Silver Strand (Rapunzel)

Once Upon a Woven Wish (Rumpelstiltskin)

Five Towers (YA Fantasy Romance)

The Sorcerer's Daughter

Highland Destiny (Paranormal Romance)

Desiring the Highland Laird

Loving the Highland Warrior (Dec 5, 2025)

Captivating the Highland Rogue (March 5, 2026)

Legends of the Five Crowns

with Misty Evans

The Lost Kingdom

The Flame and the Dragon (Coming Jan 2026)

Ransom & Fortune Adventures
(Time Travel Action/Adventure)
Highland Fling, Vol 1
Dead of Winter, Vol 2
The Citadel, Vol 3
Lord of the Underworld, Vol 4

Realm of Honor (Fantasy Romance)
One Knight Only
Only for a Knight
A Knight to Remember
A Knight Like No Other
Shadows of the Knight
Realm of Honor Collection (Books 1-5)

Shorts and Anthologies (Fantasy/Paranormal)
Newsletter Subscribers Only
A Dance Among the Faeries, A Short Story
Eorwulf, A Short Story
Dragons of Emhain Short Story Collection

Watch for more at MichelleMiles.net

ABOUT THE AUTHOR

MICHELLE MILES believes every story should have a little magic, a dash of danger, and a whole lot of heart. She writes fantasy, paranormal, and young adult adventures filled with fierce heroines, unforgettable heroes, and the kind of romance that makes you believe in happily-ever-after. From angels and demons to dragons, elves, and time travelers, her books invite readers into worlds brimming with epic quests, high stakes, and enchanting possibilities.

When she's not crafting new adventures, Michelle lends her voice to other authors' worlds as a narrator and hosts *Miles Beyond the Page*, a podcast where writers share the triumphs and challenges of their creative journeys. A proud Texan, she loves getting lost in a good book, exploring hiking trails, watching her favorite movies, and savoring a glass of wine while dreaming up her next tale.

Magical Worlds, Daring Adventures, Unforgettable Romance!

Read more at MichelleMiles.net